TO OLIVIA

READING ROCKS!

Stuart Reid (signature)

Gorgeous George

And the Incredible Iron-Bru-Man Incident

By
Stuart Reid

Illustrations, Cover and Layouts
By John Pender

Gorgeous Garage Publishing Ltd
Falkirk, Scotland

Copyright ©2019 Stuart Reid

The rights of Stuart Reid to be identified as the author of this work and the full Gorgeous George series has been asserted by him

Cover design and illustrations by John Pender
Cover and illustrations copyright © Gorgeous Garage Publishing Ltd

Photographs used by kind permission of
Betty Logan and John Pender

First Edition
This edition published in the UK by
Gorgeous Garage Publishing Ltd
ISBN 978-1-910614-12-9

www.stuart-reid.com

DEDICATION

To Eva Garland, who attends the awesome Langlands Primary School, Forfar, for her wonderful short story The Guardians, winner of the Langlands 500 Words.

You are a wonderful writer, young lady.
Keep up the good work!

To Nick Pope, former British Government Ministry of Defence official for all your information and ideas, as well as sending the U.S. Department of Defense's leaked emails. And I am sorry for creating a character in the book called Nick Poop. You deserve better.

And finally to John. This one's for you, mate.

. . . .

For my wife Angela and my little boy Lucas, whose love, encouragement and unrelenting patience means the absolute world to me.

Thank you for letting daddy live out his drawing dream!

Love always,
John xXx

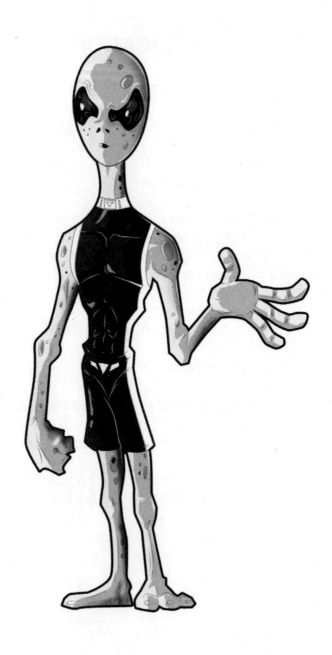

CONTENTS

"I believe alien life is quite common in the universe, although intelligent life is less so. Some say it has yet to appear on planet Earth."

Professor Stephen Hawking CH CBE FRS FRSA - Physicist, cosmologist and genius.

Chapter One - In Space

Close your eyes.

Have you opened them again? Obviously you'll have to open them again to keep reading. Okay, just imagine that you've closed your eyes. Or close them for a few seconds, then open them again, to keep reading. It's dark, isn't it?

Close your eyes again and imagine the blackest, darkest, most silent void of nothingness you can think of... and multiply it by a million. By a million billion.

And that's space. Outer space. That black space that hides behind the dark side of the moon.

Outer space is not just dark but almost the complete absence of light. Sure there are stars, tiny pin-pricks of light on the back cloth of the universe but they are so far away that you can only focus on the here and now. Or the hear and now.

But there is absolutely nothing to hear. No sound at all, as if space and time and noise have all melted together. Sound doesn't travel well in the vacuum of space.

In space no one can hear you fart.

Chapter Two - Superheroes

Boys smell!

Not just sweaty teenagers with their hormones and their spots and their greasy hair but all boys. Small boys smell too, especially when they've been running around the playground on a hot day. They come back into class after break, sweating, with their hair plastered onto their faces and steam rising up from their heads.

Girls sweat too but usually in a more delicate way. And girls smell nicer than boys because they like to spray themselves with hints of candy floss and jasmine and vanilla and sandalwood, and lots of other sweet-stinky stuff.

Basically children smell - go ask your teacher. They just smell in different ways, especially if they're hot.

And this day was a scorcher!

That's why, at that very moment, two boys were running around in the garden with their pyjamas tucked into their socks and each wearing a pair of underpants on the outside of their jim-jams.

'Weirdos!'

Allison had popped her head up over the wall at the bottom of the garden and was watching the madness unfolding on the grass below. There was a large shed to her left, a bright red kiddies' slide on her right and a paddling pool filled with water in the middle of the lawn.

The two boys were running circuits around the shed, climbing up the barrel tucked in the corner, over the shed roof, jumping back down to the grass, up the slide before finally leaping over the paddling pool.

At the top of the slide, they'd each launch themselves into the air, arms outstretched, before tucking their legs in and landing in a crouch position on the grass, one fist on the floor.

Allison was a tall girl for her age but even she had to stand on her tip-toes to see over the high wall. Her long brown hair kept blowing in her face every time she popped her head up over the brickwork but it was worth it. Well worth it, in fact, to watch those two lads running around like a couple of nut-cases. But she wanted a better look.

There was a gate along to her left, just beyond three big bins... a blue bin, a green bin and a brown bin. Recycle stuff, general rubbish and garden waste. Below the gate, steps led down to the garden, and she followed the path around. Where the bottom of the steps met the grass there were two tall trees, where Allison stood quietly. She folded her arms and smiled. This was better than television.

Occasionally one of the boys would stumble. Now and again they'd whack their knees off the barrel or the roof or slip as they climbed the slide. They were getting tired, and they were becoming careless. It was an accident waiting to happen. Allison sniggered as she pulled out her phone, clicked the 'camera' icon and waited; her thumb hovering over the red 'record' button. But she was too late.

One of the boys misjudged his jump. He fell short, one foot over the paddling pool, the other splashing down into the water, soaking his pyjama leg up to his knee. He hopped out squealing.

'It's freeeeeeeeeeeezing!' he yelped.

'You're out,' his friend laughed. 'Frazzled in the vat of toxic waste.'

'No, no, I'm fine,' cried the first boy. 'My suit protected me.' His light blue pyjamas had one dark blue leg and a soggy sock was dripping in puddles onto the grass.

Allison slipped her phone away.

'What are you two muppets playing at?' she laughed, as she walked over.

'Superheroes,' they shouted together.

'You don't look much like *Superheroes*,' giggled Allison. 'You're wearing pyjamas, George. And you've got your pants on the outside, Kenny.'

'All Superheroes wear their pants on the outside,' argued Kenny, feeling a flicker of anger bubble up inside him.

'Not all Superheroes wear their pants on the outside...' mumbled George, looking down and stubbing his toes into the grass. Allison had walked over and was now standing by the paddling pool, still smiling. She'd slipped one of her *Crocs* off and was about to dip her toes in the pool.

'Is it nice and cool?' she asked.

'I wouldn't do that, if I were you,' George smirked.

'Shh, don't tell her,' hissed Kenny. 'She was laughing at our outfits.'

'Tell her what?' asked Allison, as her foot slipped gently into the water.

'We've both been wee-ing in that pool for a couple of days!'

Chapter Three - Explanation

Right, little reader, allow me to explain. First of all, don't be upset that throughout this book I will call you 'little reader' - you are quite small after all.

Or at least I'm quite big compared to you. If you've met me, you'll know that I am nearly two metres tall. And if I've signed your book, then you were probably staring up my nose from your low vantage point.

That's okay, I am rather proud of my nose. It's quite big, and it seems to be getting bigger as I grow older. It's very hairy on the inside, you probably noticed that too. And it runs... a lot. So I hope my snot didn't drip on you or your book.

*And you probably noticed that Chapter One wasn't really a chapter at all; it was more like a prologue. Except that I didn't call it **Prologue** because some people skip the prologue, even teachers. So I had to trick you into reading it - sorry.*

But I thought it was quite a cool way to start the book. And I got to say FART on the first page!

I used to be scared of the word FART. My mum and dad would go mental if I said it, and instead, we had to say 'pump' or 'toot' or 'parp'. Then I discovered that words, and language, change from place to place. Some people get really offended by words like 'fart', whilst others think that 'fart' is just a normal word, no big deal. In one school that I've visited, teachers would say 'fart' all the time and see nothing wrong with it - after all, it's just a word. There are far more things in life to be worried about than a little fart.

And I should know because I have used the word FART in this book twenty eight times. You could count them but that would take ages, so maybe just trust me on that one. I hope this is the fartiest book ever written.

The problem is that grown-ups aren't always right, we just think we are. Or at least we try to do what we think is right. Nobody gives you a manual called HOW TO BE A GROWN-UP and you read it and suddenly, you're all grown-up. It doesn't work like that. Most grown-ups just muddle through life, making mistakes and hopefully learning from them.

Well, this book will tell you what mistakes grown-ups have made, the serious ones, and hopefully you guys will learn from them a whole lot sooner than we did!

This book contains three different sections. Chapters like this, when the words are in italics, slanted and falling over, almost too dizzy to stand up straight, written by me (the author) talking directly to you (the reader). Here, I will tell you cool stuff and scary stuff and secret stuff that you will probably find out in ten years anyway but I think you need to know sooner.

Then, there are the proper chapters, the storyline about the adventures of my characters Gorgeous George, Grandpa John, Crayon Kenny, Allison, Ben and Barbara and their discoveries about the universe. Notice, no *italics* here.

And finally, I have included quotes from real people; politicians, astronauts, scientists, statesmen and stateswomen who are much, much smarter than I am, and can say stuff in just one line that takes me two or three chapters to say. Most of these quotes are from real people with real experiences of real life. I believe we should keep our minds open, and listen to a variety of opinions, and then decide.

Other quotes are from Superheroes... and as everybody knows, Superheroes ROCK!

Right, I've kept you back from the real story. Allison has just stood in a paddling pool full of wee.

"The world is made of different races and different religions, but we're all co-travellers on the spaceship Earth and must respect and help each other along the way."

Stan Lee - Comic book writer, editor, publisher, producer, legend.

Chapter Four - Wee

'YOU WHAT!' Allison's scream was so loud and so piercing that several dogs started barking around the neighbourhood.

'You pair of disgusting mingers!' Allison's nose curled up, as if she'd just caught whiff of a particularly nasty pong. 'I'm not kidding you. Whenever I think you two could not be any more vulgar, you take things down to the next level. Vile, boys. Just vile.'

George and Kenny usually knew to take a step back whenever Allison was wound up, probably because one or both of them had been doing the winding. Today, however, Kenny was still mad at Allison laughing at his Superhero costume.

'It's not our fault,' he argued. 'The dog next door started it. We caught him widdling in the pool earlier this week. He sneaked in through the hole in the fence.'

'Crayon Kenny!' Allison slammed her hands down on her hips. 'Just because that little puppy happens to wee in the pool, it does not mean that you two need to wee in the pool too. For goodness sake, that dog licks its own bottom. Don't tell me that you've started licking your own bottoms too, have you?!'

George sniggered. He knew instantly this was a bad idea but he couldn't help himself. Allison fired him a dirty look.

And Kenny knew he was in trouble too, as soon as Allison added the insult 'Crayon' to his title. Not that it bothered him. He'd always worn 'Crayon' as a badge of honour, ever since the nurses at Little Pumpington General Hospital presented him with his very own 'silver' forceps, once they'd removed the 25th crayon from one of his nostrils. Although it should be pointed out that this was after his 25th visit to the hospital on different days, not actually removing 25 crayons on the *same* day!

Crayon Kenny was, without doubt, one of the most unpredictably idiotic boys ever to insert an object into an orifice. On a good day Kenny Roberts could be described as slightly eccentric. On other days Kenny was certified as stark raving bonkers, famous for his unusual hobby of sticking crayons, buttons, marbles, Brussel sprouts, peas and pretty much anything else up his nose, in his ears or anywhere else for that matter. George thought Kenny was hilarious!

'I'm sorry, Allison. He makes me laugh,' George conceded, handing Allison a towel. 'We were just playing.'

'What? Playing in your own wee water? Seriously?'

'And it was my Grandpa Jock's idea anyway,' shrugged George. 'He said it would add a bit of excitement and danger to our game.'

'What game, you morons?' moaned Allison. 'Why are you paddling around in a puddle of pee?'

'We were trying to avoid it, really,' admitted Kenny. 'It's not as if we wanted to put our feet in it.' Kenny gave his foot another shake and squeezed a little bit more water out of his pyjama leg.

Allison rolled her eyes to the back of her head. 'And why blame Grandpa Jock as well?'

'Technically, we could blame our parents too,' agreed George. 'We both wanted to stay home and play video games but our mums ganged up on us, said it was the hottest summer in years, and threw us outside to get some fresh air.'

'And if you haven't noticed, Allison… we've both got ginger hair!' Kenny went on. 'We've both got really pale skin. And freckles! We're going to fry this summer!'

Kenny was stating the obvious. His skin was pale, almost white beneath a dusting of speckled brown dots. If he started to count his freckles, he'd be there all day…

he knew this from experience. George, on the other hand, never tired of playing join-the-dots on his skin with a biro.

Kenny's hair was a glowing flame of amber, whilst George had a lighter shade of tangerine. 'So Grandpa Jock suggested we play at *Superheroes*,' George added. 'But not just normal Superheroes… new ones… we make them up ourselves, with cool names and new super powers.'

'Well, who are you supposed to be,' said Allison, looking Kenny up and down. 'Pyjama-man?'

'No!' snapped Kenny, before his face cracked into a smile. 'I am the Ginger Ninja!'

George explained. 'Mild-mannered Crayon Kenny here was infected by a portion of radioactive sushi from the Japanese fast food restaurant Yu-Yu-Yu! He can now move unseen and unheard, practically invisible to his enemies until it's too late.'

'And leap over a paddling pool full of wee in a single bound.' Allison giggled. She could never stay angry with these idiots for too long, even if she still felt a creeping sense of dog pee on her toes.

'Or not,' chuckled Kenny, looking down at his wet pyjama leg.

'And who are you supposed to be, George?'

'I am Stink King!'

'You're stinking? You mean you've soiled yourself again.'

George laughed. 'No, I am the Stink King, beholder of wind and banisher of bottom burps!'

'And what's your super power then?' asked Allison.

'Well, my bottom…'

'NO! I don't want to know,' cried Allison, suddenly realising her mistake. 'Anyway,' she added quickly, changing the subject. 'Where is Mr Jock?'

'Oh, he's in the shed,' nodded Kenny. 'He's been in there for a few days now.'

'A FEW DAYS! Hasn't anybody checked on him? Is he okay? What if he's had an accident?' Allison was generally a caring person, concerned about the well-being of others. The boys, on the other hand, only noticed something might be wrong if no one served them up their next meal.

'It's fine, Allison. We hear him banging and clattering every now and again,' smiled George. 'He's quiet at the moment, so he must be thinking. But his bagpipe music will soon start up.'

'He's got a CD player in there,' smiled Kenny. 'He says the tempo helps him work.'

'Seriously, you two need to think about other people for a change, not just yourselves,' Allison scolded, as she stepped across to the shed. 'Mr Jock?' She knocked on the shed door. 'Mr Jock?' She knocked again. 'Is everything okay in there?'

There was a slight pause, followed by a banging and clattering noise. It sounded like buckets and cans were being kicked aside, then the squeal of a small cat, or maybe an old man. A second later, the window around the side of the shed opened and a wrinkled old hand thrust its way out. The hand waved.

'Hey, Allison. How you doing, hen?'

'Hen? I'm not a chicken, Mr Jock,' protested Allison. 'Does #MeToo mean nothing to you?'

'That's just an old Scottish phrase Allison,' added George.

'I'm a bit busy right noo kids but ah'll no' be long. Here, have a wee drink to keep you going.'

The hand disappeared into the shed for a couple of seconds before reappearing again holding a soft drink can. Allison took it. The hand vanished again before delivering another tin. Kenny took it and the hand popped in and back out again with a third can. Allison read the label.

'Iron Brew? I've never heard of Iron Brew before?'

she said, scrunching her nose up again.

'Iron Brew!' announced a voice from inside the shed. 'IRON BREW, Scotland's other national drink, made from girders. Except we changed it to Irn Bru up north, for legal reasons.'

'It's really good,' George butted in. 'It's sweet and fizzy and blows bubbles up your nose, if you drink it too fast.'

'And you're always guaranteed a good burp afterwards,' laughed Kenny. He had obviously tried the beverage before.

'Oh aye, and give the empty cans back to me when you've finished your drinks. Ah'll need them, ye ken. Reduce, recycle, reuse! REUSE, I tell ye! There should be no *f* in *refuse*.'

And with that the hand disappeared back into the shed, quickly followed by the drone of bagpipes and an increased volume of banging, clattering and thumping.

> "There may be aliens in our Milky Way galaxy, and there are billions of other galaxies. The probability is almost certain that there is life somewhere in space."
>
> **Edwin *Buzz* Aldrin - Astronaut.**
> **Second man to walk on the moon**

CHAPTER FIVE
INTO THE DARKNESS

A LONG TIME AGO, IN A GALAXY NOT TOO FAR AWAY...

One species began to evolve. They adapted. They developed and they changed much faster than the other living creatures on that planet. By staying on top of their food chain for tens of thousands of years, without an asteroid to wipe them out, they evolved from sea creatures to amphibians to reptiles.

They rose out of the water. Fins became feet, four legs became two. Four digits evolved into three fingers and one opposable thumb. Their brains grew larger and they began to use simple tools... stone tools at first but soon more refined.

This species learned to speak and to communicate with each other in a complex pattern of sounds. They soon developed language, with strange gurgles and grunts, but this allowed for the faster spread of knowledge. Skills could be taught and shared quickly. Problem solving helped these creatures migrate across the whole planet.

And as they spread, they absorbed the land and the water and the resources of their home. They took, and took, never thinking to replace. They destroyed, never stopping to consider the effects. Their creativity to invent was only matched by their greed to consume.

These *people*, still closely related to their lizard ancestors, became the parasites of their planet. They forgot how to live in harmony with their world. Every other creature developed a natural balance with their environment, a way to live together, but not these *people*. They moved into an area and they multiplied and multiplied until every natural resource was consumed and the only way they could survive was to spread to another area.

There is another organism in the universe that follows this same pattern. It is called a virus! These creatures were a disease, a cancer of their planet. If scientists were able to classify this species, they would be a plague and there was no cure.

Lush green forests were chopped down, fossil fuels were burned, and waters became polluted. The more methane, sulphur and carbon dioxide in the atmosphere, the warmer the planet became. And every year, by burning coal, oil and gas, obscene amounts of carbon dioxide were belched into the atmosphere.

Oceans of plastic choked the once blue planet; giant landfill sites and mountains of garbage spilled into every corner of their world. Toxic waste polluted the natural world and any hope of a greener future was destroyed. Even though thousands of other species on the planet died off, no one took any notice.

Mass extinction occurred on a global scale. The planet grew warmer, and drought spread across the continents. Huge patches of land became uninhabitable. The air became unbreathable.

The last generation of this wasteland realised that their only hope of survival was to leave their dying planet. Rocket ships were built and the richest families *bought* their way off that burnt-out shell. Those that couldn't afford the price of a seat onboard were left behind to die.

And the lizard people eventually left their world to seek out a new home that could sustain them, at least for a while.

But the universe is enormous. Distances are almost unimaginable and although the Reptilian rocket ships were fast, travel across the galaxy was slow.

Generations of Reptilians grew old and died, replaced by their lizard children, then their lizard children's children. The fleet of rocket ships merged together on their voyage through space to become one gigantic colony. Their bio-domes grew larger and their food production rose. This adaptable species learned to live within the metal hulls of their rockets.

There were several stop-offs on a few small planets and moons, none of them suitable to be called *home* yet but still stripped bare of their resources. Soon, with their fuel reserves almost gone, the lizard people came to rest on a small grey rock near a larger blue planet.

By chance, this moon was spinning at exactly the same speed as the blue planet, meaning that the same side of the moon was always facing its bigger neighbour. This is known throughout the galaxy as *tidal locking*, and this moon rotates exactly once each time it circles the Earth. The lizard people chose to settle on the 'dark side of this moon', although it was just as half light and half dark as the other side, only hidden from view.

They landed their colony ships in the darkness, on the far side, knowing they would never be detected.

The bio-domes settled into the lunar dust and the Reptilians set about converting their rocket ships into landing crafts. And when they were ready, their take-over of the blue world could begin.

The mammals on the blue planet would pose no threat, even the ape-like creatures, who were all over the place.

There had been little monkeys like this on their home world but they had been easily tamed, controlled and in some cases, eaten. Until they became extinct of course.

The Reptilians, these lizard people, knew their place in this galaxy or any other galaxy. They were apex predators. They were top of the food chain. The most brutal, single-minded and savage species ever to walk on two legs. And driven by their primitive desires to satisfy their hunger, their thirst and their greed for territory. No regrets, no guilt, no emotions.

Except...

"They're here. They are parked on the side of the crater. They are watching us!"

Neil Armstrong - Astronaut. July 20th 1969.
First man to walk on the moon.

Chapter Six - Burp!

BURP!

George grinned. Kenny laughed. Allison's jaw hit the floor.

'George!' she cried. 'What do you say?'

'Probably… "Cor, that was a loud one!"' He nudged Kenny and the two boys burst into hysterics. 'The power of Iron Brew,' George nodded.

'Right, my turn,' announced Kenny, as he flipped the ring pull on the can and felt the air hiss out from underneath his finger. He knocked back his head and chugged, shaking his head as the little bubbles of fizz rippled up his nose.

'KAAAAAHHHHHH,' Kenny gulped, finally releasing the can from his mouth. One second, two seconds, three seconds…

BURP!

'We have blast off!' giggled George. 'No wonder my Grandpa Jock loves this stuff.'

'He says he grew up with it, even put it on his cornflakes when he was a kid. He says drinking Iron Brew is why his hair is a ginger colour,' George went on. 'Scotland is the only country in the world where Coca-Cola is the NOT best selling drink… it's Iron Brew! And he still drinks gallons of the stuff.'

Allison stared in amazement. She was next. She knew it, and the boys knew it, and she starting to feel a little nervous. Kenny smiled at her, a small orange moustache had formed on the corners of his mouth.

'And mind you don't spill any,' said George. 'The stains never come out.'

Allison flicked open her tin gently. She was wearing a white t-shirt and pink leggings so she was careful not to splash any. *It's only fizzy juice, it's only fizzy juice*, she kept repeating, over and over inside her head. Allison thrust the can up to her lips and gulped a mouthful.

It was fizzy, unbelievably fizzy. It was warm and tingly and the bubbles rippled around her cheeks and up her nose and all the way down into her tummy. It was hot and spicy and sweet. And ginger. Allison smacked her lips. Definitely ginger, and orange, and lemon and the cheekiest hint of more citrus and cream soda.

George and Kenny were staring at her, expectantly.

Pause…

Pause…

Suddenly, Allison let rip with the biggest belch ever in the history of burping. EVER! It thundered, it rippled, it echoed. The earth trembled. Flocks of birds swept out of trees, alarmed by the sudden noise.

If you've ever seen that film Elf, about Buddy the Elf, who's not a real elf but just a kid who crawled inside Santa's sack one Christmas and ended up at the North Pole and grew up thinking he was an elf and he went back to New York to find his dad and the bit where he drinks a whole bottle of fizzy juice really fast and then lets out a massive burp… like that. Only louder.

Dogs barked. Car alarms began bleeping. The world shuddered to a halt.

'What the heck was that?!'

A small, dark head popped up above the garden wall. Jet black hair platted into neat lines of cornrow pleats with little red and green beads at the end of each stump. Eyes dark brown, almost black. Skin dark chocolate. Smile huge.

'BEN!' The two lads cried together, delighted to see their friend.

'And what the heck are you two doing? Still dressed in your pyjamas?' Ben laughed.

George and Kenny stopped and looked down at themselves. Kenny was wearing striped pyjamas, light blue and dark blue, only one leg was now a darker, wet blue. He wore red underpants over the top and had tucked the trouser legs into a pair of skateboard kneepads. George had on his green pyjamas, tucked into brown socks, and around his waist was tied a green scarf. He was even wearing his blue pants on the outside.

'We're Superheroes! New ones, our ones,' smiled George.

'Better ones,' added Kenny. 'Look.' And he ducked behind the shed, reappearing with a plant pot in his arms. Inside was a twig, stuck into the earth.

'I am Grot,' Kenny whispered from behind the plant pot, pretending the twig was speaking.

Allison laughed. 'No, you're just grotty. Your leg stinks of dog wee!'

'It's Groot, man,' laughed Ben. 'The twig's called Groot.'

'I am Grot,' said the twig. 'We're making our own superheroes, so no copies,' said Kenny.

'And who's your sidekick George?' asked Ben excitedly.

George ran around the shed too, and brought back a black and white stuffed toy. It was very old. Originally, it might've been a panda or a badger or even a stuffed penguin (who has a stuffed badger?!) but now it just looked squished.

Proudly, George declared, 'I am Stink King and this is my sidekick, Punk the Skunk!' Allison just stared her friend. Ben looked on and smiled.

'I told you you should've called it Stinkerbelle. That's much funnier.' said Kenny.

'I did think about Rocket Raccoon or Pocket Rocket Puppy but that was kinda lame,'grinned George.

'You guys look awesome,' said Ben, his face lighting up, as if a large bulb had appeared over his head.

'We could be *Guardians of the Garden*,' he babbled. 'Avenging the vegetables, a great big Guardians Gathering, the Fantastic Five...'

'But there's only four of us,' groaned Allison. 'You're as mad as those two,' but she knew she couldn't persuade him. Ben had that same crazy look

23

in his eyes that George had sometimes.

'We could get Barbara too. She'd love to dress up.'

Barbara was Ben's twin sister. They'd moved into the house next door to Grandpa Jock last year and had already been involved in the snot zombie outbreak at Little Pumpington Primary School but that's supposed to be Top Secret.

Ben and Barbara weren't identical twins, obviously, since one of them was a boy and the other was a girl. Matching clothes would have been a problem. Barbara could've worn trousers but it might look a little odd if Ben wore a skirt, but hey, why not?! There is a certain author who is well-known for wearing his kilt all the time, and lots of kids in schools ask him *Why are you wearing a skirt?* and he has to reply *It's not a skirt, it's a kilt!* But really, if he wanted to wear a skirt, that would be okay too. Wouldn't it?

Ben ducked down behind the wall. 'Two minutes,' he shouted. 'Just give me two minutes!'

As quick as The Flash, Ben was back in his garden again,

climbing over the wall to join the other kids. He looked sleek. He looked smooth, and he moved with a cat-like elegance. Landing on all-fours, he bounced up on his feet and flicked his hands out. Lowering his voice, he growled…

'I am Black Puma!'

'Awesome!' cried George

'Cool,' cried Kenny.

'Are those your mum's pyjamas?' asked Allison, raising both eyebrows. 'They look quite silky. I don't think she'll be happy, Ben.' But Ben wasn't listening. He was too busy leaping over the paddling pool with George and Kenny.

Was it a spell? Were these boys infected with the same type of madness? Or was is just stupidity? Allison couldn't be sure but something had caused these lads to prance about the garden in weird outfits.

And Ben was definitely wearing his mum's jim-jams. Black satin trousers and top, the matching type; the kind that mums sometimes wear on a Saturday night (but who knows why?). They were sleek and very shiny and he'd tucked them into a pair of dark socks and covered his face with a black cat mask… like a panther's.

CRASH!

The door of the shed smashed open and all four children jumped back. Ben, with his cat-like reflexes jumped the furthest. George jumped into Allison's arms and Kenny jumped into the paddling pool again, soaking his other leg.

An orange and blue robot stepped into the garden!

25

> # "Tony Stark was able to built this in a cave! With a box of scrap!"
>
> **Obadiah Stane, Iron Monger - from Iron Man**

Chapter Seven - Fourth Wall

Hey, it's me again. Sorry for butting in but I thought I should mention the reason why I like talking directly to you like this. It's called First Person, *where I am the author talking directly to YOU the reader. It's kinda like playing on a video game, like Minecraft or COD*, where it feels like 'This is my arm, this is my sword or my gun, and this is my adventure'.*

The real story in this book, the proper plot, is told in Third Person, where she does this, and he does that, and they do something else.

And me talking to you in first person like this is also called 'Breaking Down the Fourth Wall'.

Imagine this book contains hidden knowledge and every single page is a big box, with not just three dimensions but four. Deep inside every page, hidden between the words, is an enormous cavern of knowledge and it's up to you, the reader, to discover those secrets.

*It's like when I am on stage at a book festival or in a school, there is a barrier between me and the audience, and I need to break down the barrier in order to bring everyone along on the adventure. Me talking directly to you in first person like this helps breaks down that barrier…
that fourth wall.*

Oh, and while you're here, I mentioned earlier that this book is three books in one - the main story, the author bits and the quotes.

Well, I've been thinking… you probably paid about seven quid for this book, which is a great price, but technically, it's THREE books so maybe you should've paid closer to £20 for it… that's only fair. If you agree, go ask your mum or dad for one of their credit cards, visit my website **www.stuart-reid.com** and upload the extra cash, like a donation or something. Thank you!

*And yeah, I mentioned COD earlier… yeah Call of Duty… big deal. So what! It's a video game series and it also has an `18 certificate` so you're too young to play it but I know you probably do anyway. Grown-ups argue about this stuff all the time. As I've said before, there are far more important things in the world that grown-ups need to get really angry about, instead of worrying about stupid video games.

** And I was only kidding about the online donation thing earlier. DON'T upload your mum and dad's credit card details onto any website. Ever. EVER!

*** And finally, I can't believe I got through a full chapter without writing 'FART'.

**** Finally, finally… get back to the story. It's Grandpa Jock's big arrival

Chapter Eight - Arrival

The ground seemed to shake as the shed door slammed back on its hinges. The screeching wail of bagpipes blasted from inside the hut and ended with a triumphant *TA-DAH!*

Standing before them was a small tin man with wisps of ginger hair sprouting out from beneath his face mask. His suit looked muscular, with powerful shoulders and a broad chest made out of soda cans. His arms and legs were also wrapped in aluminium, sprayed orange and blue but you could just see brand names shining beneath.

In the centre of his chest was a bright blue light, which dazzled anyone who looked directly into it.

'Can anyone join your super-secret boy band?' echoed a voice from inside the metal suit. Slowly and robotically, its right hand raised up to its helmet and fingers flipped the visor. A fluffy orange moustache, a big grin and a pair of twinkling eyes appeared.

'GRANDPA!' shouted George, untangling himself from Allison's grasp.

'Mr Jock!' cried Kenny, Allison and Ben together.
'You look amazing!' said Ben.

'You look like Iron Man,' added Kenny.

'Iron Man? I like that,' nodded Grandpa Jock. 'That's kind of catchy. It's got a nice ring to it. I mean it's not technically accurate. The suit's made from old tin cans but it's kinda provocative, the imagery anyway.'

'Are those Iron Brew cans, Mr Jock?' asked Allison, pointing at the tins strapped to his legs. The soft drink branding was clearer here, not entirely covered over.

'Yeah, I kinda ran out of paint,' shrugged Grandpa Jock. 'Is it obvious? Some of them were orange flavour and others were cola but most of the tins were Iron Brew.'

'Iron Brew? Iron Bru! That's it!' yelled George. 'You can be Iron-Bru-Man! That's your superhero name, Grandpa.'

'George, you're a marvel. Well done, lad.' Grandpa Jock began strutting back and forth across the garden, stopping, turning and posing majestically. Now and again, he would drop down onto one knee and punch the grass, digging up little tufts of turf with his tin knees.

'That man has no regard for lawn maintenance,' huffed Allison, as she stepped back against the shed.

'Superheroes, assemble!' he shouted, and George, Kenny and Ben were keen to join in the group pose. The boys jumped forward, fists in the air, arms clenched, eyebrows down, looking dangerous. Grandpa Jock stopped.

'Hang on, lassie. Are you no' playing with us then?' Grandpa Jock called across to Allison.

Allison hesitated. At first she'd thought the boys were just being silly but actually, dressing up looked a lot of fun. It was definitely better than just standing around watching.

'I didn't know, Mr Jock,' she replied. 'I don't have an outfit.'

'Go round to my house,' cried Ben. 'Barbara's in there. She'd love to be a superhero.'

'But I thought it was only boys that could be superheroes,' piped Kenny. Allison could feel the hairs on the back of her neck rising up.

'Don't be ridiculous, Crayon. Girls can be better superheroes than boys,' snapped Allison. 'We'll be Super-Sheroes!' And she turned and walked up the steps to Grandpa Jock's back garden gate.

She didn't intend to climb the wall, like Ben did, at least not until she had her superhero costume on. So she flipped the latch and walked over to the gate next door. Then she stopped abruptly.

The world seemed to buzz and crackle. The image before her eyes zoomed in and out of focus. A cold shiver of fear rippled down her back. Behind her, she could hear the boys arguing, their voices dull and distant.

'We can be the Guardians of the Galaxy,' Ben cried.

'That name's been taken, Ben. We've got to invent new ones.'

George added. 'We're just Guardians of the Garden then.'

'What about Guardians Get-Together,' laughed Kenny. 'That's almost as good as Avengers Assemble. Isn't it?'

'Are you mad?' sniggered Ben. 'Guardians Get-Together sounds more like tea-party!'

'How cool would it be to actually guard the galaxy!?'

The voices became quieter, empty echoes at the back of her mind. Her eyes were glued to the vision in front of her, nothing else seemed to matter. Allison lifted her hand, trembling and she covered her mouth with it. She wanted to scream but the noise stuck in her throat. She wanted to run but she had no control over her legs.

Across the road, beyond the trees and down toward the fields, there hovered a large saucer-shaped object. It was round and silver with a ring of flashing lights around the base. It made no noise, other than a distant hum, and the air beneath the craft seemed to shimmer. It was moving slowly left to right, then right to left, as if it was searching for something.

It was too quiet to be a helicopter, and it had no rotor-blades. It was moving too slowly to be an aeroplane. Weather balloons have no lights beneath them. This wasn't a trick of the light. This wasn't an odd-shaped cloud. This wasn't swamp gas. This thing was solid, and distinct, and moving in a pattern. Occasionally, beams of green light flashed out from the base of the craft and scanned the ground the below.

Allison was a sensible girl. She wasn't prone to fancy

flights of imagination. She liked science and evidence and practical, down-to-earth explanations. She liked to keep her feet firmly planted in reality. But what she was seeing was beyond belief.

Should she scream? Should she shout out? Was she alone in seeing this? Other witnesses would be good but perhaps her voice would alert the craft and it would shoot off, leaving her looking foolish. All these thoughts flew around her head in micro-seconds, as time seemed to stand still.

'Are you okay there, lassie?' A voice from the garden shook her back into the real world and she turned to see Grandpa Jock climbing up the steps in his iron can suit. 'I didnae see you go next door, and I wondered where you…'

Grandpa Jock's voice trailed off as he reached the top of the stairs. He followed Allison's gaze across the wooded area and nodded.

'You see it too, don't you?' asked Allison, desperate to know she wasn't going mad, that she wasn't just seeing things. 'Tell me you see it, Mr Jock.'

'Aye, lassie, they're here,' nodded Grandpa Jock. 'I've been expecting them.'

"UFOs are as real as the airplanes flying overhead"

Paul Hellyer, former Canadian Minister of National Defence

Chapter Nine - Reptilians

At that very moment, on the other side of the moon, a large, black spacecraft was lifting off. There was no fire or exhaust fumes or plumes of smoke, just a gentle cloud of lunar dust blowing in low gravity. It hovered for a few seconds over the surface of the moon, before spinning outwards at tremendous speed, orbiting around and setting off towards the blue planet.

This craft was enormous. A huge, dark triangle with glowing orbs of bright, white light in each of the three corners. And it flew through space at an incredible speed.

On board this ship were two hundred Reptilians; the most brutal, vicious and heartless species of creature ever before seen in the galaxy. Their value system was based on strength, greed and pure ruthlessness. Taking everything they could, whenever they wanted, and never worrying about the cost.

They were the apex predators; top of the food chain. Driven by their primitive desires to satisfy their hunger, their thirst and their greed for territory, with no regrets, no guilt, no emotion...

Except...

They liked a good fart!

Farting was at the heart of their civilisation. It was nature's calling card, in both sound and smell. The ability to fart louder than any other reptile in their colony was always a major step up the chain of command.

Taking pride in the most basic of animal functions set them apart from every other species in the galaxy. They depended on it. They thrived on it. With a diet of mostly meat, these creatures needed to expel the build up of bowel gas. And they did it with great pleasure.

They learned to harness their methane gas and this wind power became the cornerstone of their success. Burning their bottom burps produced enormous amounts of energy, and the species thrived.

Known as the Dracos, or Lizard People, or Reptilians, they had spread throughout the galaxy, in small pockets of survivors after the destruction of their home world.

Many thousands of years before, they lived on a planet in the Draco system several light years away from Earth. Their skin was green and scaly, they had four claws on each hand, and their teeth were small but very sharp. Their eyes were large, with long dark slits instead of pupils. These slits provided a wide depth-of-vision, making the Dracos excellent ambush hunters, when they dragged their lizard-like bodies out of the seas, many generations ago.

They had developed large brains. They created language, and at first, spoke using gurgles and growls from the back of their throats. Then the sound came from the back of their brains. Their large brains created telepathic connections.

They once had strong tails but these had evolved into small, green stumps on their bottoms. In another million years or so, those useless bony butts would be gone.

And this species was neither male nor female; everyone was the same. There was only one gender. Everyone could bear offspring, although they fed their babies by barfing up food, just the same as birds do on Earth.

At times of great hardship, or if their leaders wanted to purify the species' bloodlines, the old, the sick or the injured would be killed and eaten by the rest of the tribe. No mercy was shown. Indeed, it was accepted as a noble sacrifice to be eaten by your family, to give strength and nourishment and extra wind power to the next generation. And they grew stronger.

Strong enough to launch their first raiding party towards the big blue planet. Their time to conquer Earth had finally arrived.

"I saw this illumination moving with respect to the stars. We were smart enough to not say 'Houston, there's a light out there that's following us.' So, technically, it becomes an unidentified flying object."

Edwin Buzz Aldrin - Astronaut. Second man to walk on the moon.

Chapter Ten - Close Encounters of the First Kind

'You see it too, right?' Allison nudged the old Scotsman beside her. 'Tell me you see it.'

'Aye, lassie, they're here,' nodded Grandpa Jock. 'I've been expecting them.'

'Expecting them?' gasped Allison. 'Expecting who?'

'Been expecting them for years...'

The round saucer-shaped craft was still hovering beyond the trees, unaware of their presence. Grandpa Jock's back gate faced across a narrow road towards the wooded area beside a field. Next to the field was a large lake. The surface of the water occasionally rippled as the unidentified flying object shifted from the trees to the lake and back again.

'Something's wrong,' growled Grandpa Jock. 'They're not landing. They're searching.'

Beams of light shone down between the trees, and even in the bright afternoon sunshine the wood seemed to throb and pulse with a glow of green energy. The craft darted back and forth, forward and back, in a grid-like pattern.

'Is that... is that... a UFO?' stammered Allison, her eyes never leaving the hovering object.

Grandpa Jock chuckled. 'Well, yeah, I suppose. We've no idea what that object really is and it's flying doon there so you could say it's pretty much unidentified.'

'I'm being serious, Mr Jock!' snapped Allison, a slight quiver in her voice. She knew he was trying to pull her leg and wasn't going to stand for it. 'Is that a flying saucer?'

Grandpa Jock's face straightened. Allison was shocked but not exactly frightened or alarmed. Maybe now was as good a time as any for full disclosure.

'Yeah, you are correct, young lady,' he drawled.
'But we prefer to call them Unidentified Aerial Phenomenon these days.'

The government was always worried that the public would panic if news of unidentified flying objects was released. In 1938, a radio show called *War of the Worlds* broadcast a play about aliens landing in New Jersey. The actors made the play sound like real news but some people tuned in late, and missed the *'It's only a play'* announcement at the start.

People thought that Martians were actually invading and mass panic spread across the north east of America! Police were swamped with calls from people in different locations, terrified by what they'd heard. One man was believed to have had a heart attack caused by the play. Afterwards, it was reported that the country was 'frightened… almost of out its wits.'

The main narrator of the play, an actor called Orson Welles, apologised to the country on radio, saying 'We used real cities in America. I anticipated nothing unusual. Of course, I'm terribly sorry now.'

Then, on the 9th July 1947, the Roswell Daily Record flashed this headline across the front of its newspaper…

RAAF Captures Flying Saucer On Ranch in Roswell Region

Roswell Army Air Field public information officer Walter Haut issued a press release stating that personnel from the 509th Operations Group had recovered a flying disc, which had crashed on a ranch near Roswell. The press release, picked up by numerous outlets, read…

"The many rumours regarding flying discs became reality yesterday when the intelligence office of the Eighth Air Force, Roswell Army Air Field, was fortunate enough to gain possession of a disc through the cooperation of one of the local ranchers and the sheriff's office of Chaves County."

This was an unauthorised mistake! They changed their minds, so they changed their story. The military decided to conceal the true purpose of the crashed device, informing the public that the crash was, in fact, *NOT* a UFO. Another news release was issued, this time from the Fort Worth base, and later that day, the Commanding General of the Eighth Air Force, Roger Ramey stated that it was just a weather balloon that had been recovered. The military wanted to end the rumours quickly, and "the story died the next day".

However, in the years that followed, leaked reports from official insiders stated that at least one alien spacecraft crashed near Roswell, alien bodies had been recovered, and a government cover-up had taken place.

By coincidence (or perhaps not), just a few weeks later, United States President Harry S. Truman signed the National Security Act of 1947, creating the US Air Force, the Central Intelligence Agency and the National Security Council.

There are lots of rumours too, that President Truman also issued an executive order to his Secretary of Defense* James Forrestal to set up a top secret group called Operation Majestic Twelve. This blue-ribbon panel of scientists, government and military officials was also known as MJ-12. They were tasked with the cover-up of all and any UFO discoveries.

One Truman military aide, Robert B. Landry, admitted he was asked to give Truman a quarterly verbal report on UFOs from 1948 to 1952.

Then, in 1952, Truman was so alarmed by multiple sightings of UFOs over Washington that he oversaw the creation of the National Security Agency. The NSA is still the national level intelligence agency of the Department of Defense*, and they collected mass data worldwide on the existence of UFOs. However, it was so secret that insiders described the NSA as No Such Agency.

The following year, when Dwight D. Eisenhower became president, the MJ-12 committee and the NSA eventually set up a meeting between space aliens and the president. In 1954, President Eisenhower reached an agreement which allowed a group of aliens to study human biology via abductions and animal mutilations. This was in exchange for use of extraterrestrial "black" technology that would lead to developments like the B-2 "Stealth Bomber."

In Britain, we spell Defence with a 'c' but Americans use an 's' as in Defense. It drives me bonkers. Don't get me started about words like COLOR - it's just laziness to drop vowels!

> ## "I can assure you that flying saucers, given that they exist, were not constructed by any power on Earth."
>
> **Harry S. Truman - 33rd President of the United States of America**

'What do you mean "it's searching", Mr Jock? How do you know?' asked Allison, never taking her eyes off the spaceship.

'I've been on board one of those things,' nodded Grandpa Jock, his face so serious that Allison knew instantly he wasn't joking.

'Seriously?' she gasped. 'You've been on board a flying saucer?'

'Yeah, long time ago,' he sighed. 'And it wasn't pretty.'

On and on, the craft bounced left and right, back and forth, in sharp, jerky movements. It wasn't exactly small, perhaps the size of bus but in a classic saucer shape with a dome on top and flashing lights around the base.

Grandpa Jock and Allison stared forward intently, losing track of time, hypnotised by the strange object. But the air was suddenly shattered by a screaming rush of noise and wind, as two black jets raced across the sky in front of them. They were passed so fast, even before the two witnesses could turn their heads. Then, the planes were gone, right to left, and banking sharply upwards, trails of white, hot exhaust gases blasting behind them.

Allison's ears were still buzzing, and Grandpa Jock felt his false teeth rattle in his mouth before he clamped his gums down tightly.

'What was that?' gasped Allison, her voice sounding dull and echoey inside her head.

'The first wave,' nodded the old Scotsman. 'And here's their back-up.'

Off to the right, away in the distance, Allison could just make out two jet black helicopters approaching menacingly. Each had huge blades spinning above the roof of the chopper, and the body was slung low with rows of missiles. It seemed odd but to Allison, they looked angry.

Directly ahead, the flying saucer had stopped, hovering silently above the trees. With a swirl and a ripple of light, the craft spun around and took off away from them. Within two seconds the saucer was gone, vanished into the upper atmosphere.

Chapter 11 - Close Encounters of the Second Kind

Grandpa Jock clunked and clanked back into the garden, his tin suit clattering together as fast as his old legs could carry him. Allison ran behind, still not sure what they'd just seen and where they were now going. But the old geezer was on a mission.

'You gather the lads together,' yelled Grandpa Jock over his shoulder. 'I need to collect something from my shed.'

Without another word, he bombed down the last few steps, sprinted across the grass and leapt, two footed, over the paddling pool. Of course, he was weighed down by the ungainly tin cans strapped across his body, around his legs and his arms. And he was seventy four years old, or eighty two or even ninety six, or whatever age the old geezer was rumoured to be - not even he knew.

So, as might be expected, his leap over the paddling pool wasn't quite successful. He landed at the far side with a splash, and without breaking stride, he ran onwards, ducked left and disappeared inside his shed. A trail of water splattered the slabs on the other side of the grass.

'The paddling pool's full of wee, Grandpa. You might not want... oh never mind,' groaned George, never surprised by his grandfather's antics. Sometimes it was easier just to accept things. Allison had reached the grass and was calling over to the boys.

'George! George! Did you know that your Grandpa says he's has been on board a flying saucer?' She was breathless with excitement.

'Yeah, probably,' George shrugged. 'My mum says that he makes up lots of things but it wouldn't surprise me if he had.'

'And we've just seen one!' she squealed.

'Seen what?' asked Ben, stepping around the paddling pool.

'A UFO! A flying saucer! An unidentified flying object,' she went on. 'A space ship... what did he call them... unidentified aerial phenomenon!'

'Phe-nom-en-on... do doooo dee doo doo... phe-nom-en-on... do doo deee dood.' Kenny chuckled to himself at he sang his little ditty.

'You're the muppet, Kenny,' Allison snapped. 'We've just seen a space ship over there and I think Mr Jock wants us to investigate. There's also two jets and two helicopters and goodness knows what else down in the woods. This is no time for your nonsense.'

Grandpa Jock could always count on Allison to grab the boys attention. Kenny's mouth snapped shut, he stopped smiling and took a moment to let Allison's words sink in.

'We heard the jets, Allison. They sounded really cool,' said Ben, lifting the cat mask off his head. 'But space ships... that's a bit mad, don't you think?'

'Not ships! A ship! One ship... one space ship. It took off in a flash, faster than anything I've ever seen before.' Allison was flicking her fingers and waving her arm in a zooming motion. 'And the helicopters are still there.'

'Well, what are we waiting for? Let's go,' urged George, turning towards the steps.

'Hold on, hold on' A gruff Scottish voice panted behind them. 'Your mothers will kill me if I get you lot into trouble. I know what I'm dealing with but you guys? Not so sure.'

'Come on, Grandpa. Allison says the flying saucer flew off.' George was already on the third step.

'And I'd love to see the helicopters,' added Ben, joining George on the stairs.

Grandpa Jock loved a good adventure. As a boy, he was always climbing trees and exploring the open fields and green forests near his home in Scotland. In those days, children were sent off to play by themselves and often, were never seen until they felt hungry or it got dark, which ever came first.

The Scotsman always tried to install this sense of excitement into his grandson. Although the old geezer enjoyed playing games on his Playstation (yeah, even old people can play video games!) or on George's X-Box, he felt they were often empty and unsatisfying; their victories hollow and short-lived.

He loved jumping down from the battle bus for a full-on military assault onscreen but it couldn't beat the real thing. And Grandpa Jock had done the real thing many times.

So, as the old man and the four youngsters crossed the road and headed down towards the woods, he felt confident he could manage any situation. Both helicopters were still buzzing high above the tree tops but the forest was big enough that they could slip in beneath unnoticed.

Sadly, the wooded area was neither open or green. Nobody would want their children to play there. Like many off-road areas around this country, it had become the town's unofficial rubbish tip.

There were old sofas, burst mattresses and bags of rubbish lying all over the place. Where the road met the edge of the trees, piles of junk were discarded in ugly heaps. Clearly, cars and trucks had simply pulled over, opened their doors and heaved their rubbish out.

'What a pigging dump!' grunted Kenny.

'Some people are just too lazy to drive to the proper council tip,' moaned Allison, stepping over a rusty old bike.

'Watch your feet everybody. There's a lot of dog mess about here,' groaned Grandpa Jock, carefully placing his feet between the little piles of poop. In places the grass was so overgrown that watching out for hidden piles of doggy-doo-doo was a full time job. One wrong move might mean a mucky mess on your shoes.

At least the boys had put their shoes on… standing in a pile of dog poo in your socks was just too horrible for words. But, having said that, nobody wants to get dog poo in between the grooves on the soles of their trainers. It's either in there for weeks or you have to scrape it out with an old knife. Dragging your foot over the grass or against the edge of a kerb never quite gets it all out.

The wooded area opened out down towards the pond. This might have been a beautiful, secluded picnic area had it not been for the barrels of oil, more bags of waste, an old fridge, two more mattresses and another sofa dumped at the water's edge.

Don't even think about the mattresses! Brown and yellow stains covered the cloth surface and those marks had probably been there before it was trashed. And not just one stain… loads of stains. Top, middle, bottom… bottom? BOTTOM STAINS! It's frightening to think about the number of people who wet their beds again and again, and just change the sheets on the top, forgetting about the build up of bacteria underneath. They probably think it's easier to turn their mattress over and forget about that 'accident' - until the next time!

The water was a murky brown colour with a scum of floating debris littering the edges; tin cans, crisp packets and small bits of rubbish. The sofa was half in and half out of the water. Dampness was creeping up the old cloth border with a high tideline, almost up to the cushions, once flowery and quaint, now filthy.

And the stink! Even STINK would say the pond stunk! The muddy brown water had been left to fester in the warm sunshine and the air around the pond was ripe.

'And I thought you were the Stink King, George?' laughed

Ben, waving his hand across his face. 'This place honks!'

'Heads up, kids. They're back again.' Grandpa Jock was pointing up to the blue sky beyond the trees. Two black helicopters were headed back to the woods, flying low and heavy above the fields. The kids had almost forgot why they were searching down there. Only Allison had the seen the flying saucer, and for the boys, it was just a wild goose chase. They'd heard the jets but they were long gone. The helicopters looked pretty cool though.

Until they stopped directly above the pond! They were huge… and terrifying… and very, very noisy. Grandpa Jock and the children may well have been shouting but beneath the blades, nobody could hear each other. Ripples of water splashed outwards, as the surface of the pond was whipped up by the downdraft. Everyone covered their mouths and eyes, scared to ingest the filth.

George and Kenny stumbled behind the sofa, trying to shield themselves from the spray. Ben, Allison and Grandpa Jock darted back for the tree line. The helicopters still hovered there for a few moments, watching and waiting, before swivelling and arcing away towards the horizon.

Everyone's ears were still buzzing when George shouted across 'Grandpa, what did you see down here?'

'It was a close encounter, George,' Grandpa Jock yelled back. 'Of the First Kind.'

'What's a *close encounter*?' asked Ben, stepping out from behind the trees with Grandpa Jock and Allison.

'A close encounter is when a person comes into contact with an unidentified flying object,' Grandpa Jock replied.

'And what do you mean *first kind*, Mr Jock?' asked Kenny, still crouching behind the sofa.

'A close encounter of the first kind is just seeing a UFO from a distance,' Grandpa Jock replied.

'Grandpa? What's the *second kind*?' George's voice held a slight quiver. He was looking down at the sofa.

'A close encounter of the second kind would be the discovery of *evidence* of a UFO, like scorch marks on the ground.' Grandpa Jock was staring intently at the boys.

'Is this what you would call *evidence*, Mr Jock?' And Kenny stepped back from the sofa to reveal a small grey alien climbing out from beneath the cushions.

Chapter 12 - Close Encounters of the Third Kind

The alien, and it was very obviously *alien*, stepped clear of the sofa and up onto the dry grass. It was small, less than one metre in height, with long, spindly arms and short skinny legs.

Its head was huge, compared to its body, shaped like an almond, with two large, black eyes in the middle. The eyes never blinked but they were soft, with a mischievous twinkle. The alien had no obvious ears, two tiny little dots for nostrils and small slit mouth.

Its skin was grey and pale, and the alien wore a tight-fitting suit that merged into every contour of its body.

Nobody said a word. Everyone just stared at the extraterrestrial, and the little ET stared back at them. Its hairless eyebrows curled upwards and its chin began to quiver. Allison was first to react.

'Awww... look at his little face,' she said. 'He's just scared.' Allison crouched down and crawled slowly forward across the grass.

'Hey, little guy, don't be scared,' she cooed. 'You're so cute.' She held out her hand to stroke the alien's face…

Suddenly, the tiny slit mouth, almost too small to see, seemed to split the creature's head wide open, exposing two rows of vicious teeth. The alien's head bobbed forward with a snarl and snapped shut, just short of Allison's fingers.

RARRRRRR!

Allison jumped back with a yelp.

'What are you doing?' yelled the alien. 'Are you trying to give me a disease? Do you know how easy it is to get infected in this dump? Do you have dog poo on your hands? You were crawling around there, you put your hands down on the grass. You might have dog poo on your fingers.'

'But you nearly bit my finger off,' Allison was facing up to (well, down to) the little grey figure and shouting. Grandpa Jock took a step forward and placed a hand on her shoulder. The boys were frozen to the spot… Fear? Shock? Stunned silence? Who could tell?

'Look, I'm sorry,' shrugged the alien, holding its palms upwards. 'I didn't mean to snap at you. I gave you a scare, I apologise. But, I mean, you guys live with disease and dog poo all around you. This is all new for me. And I've seen humans do it, you pick dog poo up with your hands. You put it in little plastic bags. You walk around with bags of dog poo, swinging them in the air. Some of you weirdos hang the plastic bags on branches, like you're making a poo-tree or something!'

'Why is he speaking in an American accent?' whispered Kenny, still holding onto George's elbow.

'Why do think, bozo?' snapped the alien. 'You guys have been blasting television signals out there into the universe for seventy or eighty years, most of the shows are American. Most of the shows are repeats, or reruns. Over and over… repeats, repeats, repeats. The same shows again and again and again. And boy, do you guys like the sound of your own voices? That's all we hear up there!'

This time it was Ben who stepped forward. 'I won't shake your hand, if you'd rather not but, I suppose I should say *Welcome to Earth*, man.'

'You're right, dude. Fist bump will do.' The alien clenched his hand and held it out. Ben pounded knuckles with the alien, and the little grey guy did the same with Allison, Kenny and George. They each said their name in turn. Only Grandpa Jock stood back a little. The alien turned towards Kenny now.

'Okay dude, didn't mean to snap at you too.' The alien's head bobbed back and forth apologetically. 'Shouldn't have called you *bozo* either. But, I mean, I've never been abandoned on an alien planet before, thirty-nine light years from home. I'm a little stressed here. A little *spaced out*, if you like.'

'What do you mean *alien planet*?' Allison began. 'You're the alien here.'
'Okay, okay, technically I am the extraterrestrial in this situation but from my world this planet is alien to me. I mean, totally alien… weird, you know. I've already mentioned the poo-trees! Listen you

guys, just call me Stan-Ley. I am from a planet in the Zeta Reticula system.'

'I know,' said Grandpa Jock quietly. 'I've met your father. It's Dorian, isn't it? Does he still collect cow farts?'

'You know my dad?' squealed the little alien. 'Holy shizzle-sticks, dude! That's amazing. How do you know my dad?'

'We first met a long time ago,' smiled Grandpa Jock. 'Well, *met* is not entirely accurate. I sneaked aboard his spaceship dressed up as a pantomime cow once.'

'Wow! That was a long time ago,' laughed Stan-Ley. 'We stopped using methane as a power source decades ago. We just thought it would be funny if your scientists tried to back-engineer cow fart technology.'

'He said I should show you this, if I ever bumped into you guys again.' And Grandpa Jock held up a small pebble. It was a dark red colour, smooth and oval. The stone had three circles carved on one side… not carved into the stone but carved out, embossed.

The pebble's background circle surrounded a square, and was overlapped by the two smaller circles, which were both inscribed with a crescent and a circle.

'Whoa, dude! Seriously! Is that a Commander's Calling Card? I've heard about those things but I've never seen one. You must be older than you look!' Stan-Ley's already huge eyes were almost popping out of his enlarged head.

It was George's turn to step forward. He'd been listening quietly, almost having to hold Kenny up, as his knees seemed to have buckled at the sight of an extraterrestrial.

'Hold on… sorry, everybody. I'm having a hard time with all this,' he said, one puzzled eyebrow pointing upwards. 'You're an alien from a galaxy called Zeta something? And you, Grandpa, somehow know his dad? That's some story.'

Chapter 13 - Your Planet - the serious bit

The little alien dude is right. Our planet is a mess!

There are floating plastic islands in the pacific ocean that are four times larger that the British isles... bigger than the state of Texas. This whole area is called the Great Pacific Garbage Patch.

Humans have been dumping rubbish into the ocean for thousands of years but in 1950, the world's population of 2.5 billion produced 1.5 million tons of plastic. Now we have a global population of more than 7 billion people and we produce over 320 million tons of plastic. And this is set to double by the year 2034.

Every day eight million pieces of plastic pollution find their way into our oceans. Thirteen billion plastic bottles are dumped every year.

There may now be over five trillion macro and micro-plastic pieces floating in the open seas and this junk pile weighs almost 300,000 tonnes. This is more than 10 blue whales, or 43 Eiffel Towers, or 150 elephants!

Plastic pollution can now be found on every beach in the world, from busy tourist beaches to uninhabited, tropical islands. Nowhere is safe! And scientists have recently discovered micro-plastics embedded deep in the Arctic ice.

The worldwide fishing industry dump an estimated 150,000 tons of plastic into the ocean each year, including packaging, plastic nets, lines, and buoys.

We are choking the world with plastic and doing nothing to stop it.

It takes about 450 years just for one plastic bottle to break down in the ground! 11% of household waste is plastic, and 40% of that waste is plastic bottles. Plastic bags and other plastic garbage thrown into the ocean kill as many as one million sea birds every year. More than 100,000 marine mammals and turtles are killed by plastic pollution every single year. Recent studies have revealed marine plastic pollution in 100% of marine turtles, 59% of whales, 36% of seals and 40% of seabird species examined. The stuff is everywhere.

And every year we make enough plastic to shrink-wrap California!

Recycling one tonne of plastic bottles would save 1.5 tonne of carbon, stopping carbon from polluting our atmosphere. One tonne of plastic is the same as 25,000 PET plastic bottles.

The PET part of the name stands for Poly-Ethylene Terephthalate - What the fudge! Even the name sounds poisonous.

But the good news is that we can recycle plastic bottles. Just 25 PET bottles can be used to make an adult's fleece jacket. Plastic bottles can be recycled to make carpets and even road surfaces. There are over 1,000km of roads in China that are made entirely from reclaimed plastics.

And in developing nations, empty PET bottles can be filled with water and left in the sun to allow the water to be disinfected by ultra-violet radiation. So, the sun can even clean our water for us.

But the most shocking snippet of info is that nearly every piece of plastic EVER made still exists today!

And that's a good story to tell your grandchildren… if the human race lives long enough to have grandchildren.

"To me, writing is fun. It doesn't matter what you're writing, as long as you can tell a story."

Stan Lee - Comic book writer, editor, publisher, producer, legend.

Chapter 14 - First Contact

'That's some story, Grandpa,' said George, his eyebrows arching upwards.

'A story, eh? You've no' heard anything yet lad.' Grandpa Jock wiggled both his bushy eyebrows in return. 'But first, I think we need to get this little guy to safety before those helicopters come back.'

The old Scotsman led the way with the little alien tucked in behind him; the youngsters forming a guard of honour around him at the back. They stepped carefully through the forest, around the heaps of garbage and piles of poo, across the road and down into Grandpa Jock's back garden. A girl was standing on the grass in her pink fluffy pyjama bottoms and an enormous red t-shirt.

She was about ten years old. Her dark, ebony skin was smooth and flawless and seemed to shine in the sunlight. Her brown eyes were sharp but her brows were knotted. She stood with her hands on her hips, staring up at the group as they came down the steps.

'Ben Huss! You are in so much trouble, bro,' she yelled. 'Mama's gonna go mad when she finds out you haven't done your homework, boy.'

She went on. 'Here's me, staying in and studying like a good little nerd because in fifteen years time, I want to be one of the greatest minds of the 21st century. But you, wasting your time dressing up with… Shoot, dawg! What is that?'

The girl stopped in mid-sentence, distracted by the small grey figure that had stepped out from behind Grandpa Jock. Ben trotted up for a couple of paces to answer his sister.

'Barbara, meet Stan-Ley. He's from Zeta Reticula.' Ben's big grin was disarming, and he liked catching his sister off-guard. She was just too smart sometimes.

'Is that a freaking alien? Dude, that is just cray-cray!'
Barbara squealed, totally forgetting about any homework
assignments that were due.

'Cray cray? Is she feeling alright?' asked Grandpa Jock,
vaguely aware that young people spoke in a different
language sometimes.

'Don't worry Mr Jock,' Allison reassured him. 'It's just
short for 'crazy'.'

'Crazy is right,' Barbara yelled, pointing at the alien.
'He is just too cute.'

'Don't get too close, Barbara. He bites,' giggled Ben, and
Allison looked at her fingers again. They were all still there.

'Only when some kids are about to stick their poop-
covered little fingers in my mouth,' complained Stan-Ley,
holding out his spindly arms to ask for support. 'Nobody
wants to eat poop, okay. So, old dude? When did you first
meet my dad?"

'It was way back in 1947,' shrugged Grandpa Jock.
'I had sneaked on board his spaceship then, may even have
caused it to crash… near Roswell, New Mexico. I said sorry
to him later though. He was cool with it.'

Stan-Ley just nodded. All five youngsters stood with their
mouths open wide.

'You were on board a spaceship, Mr Jock?' Ben's eyes
were popping out of his head.

'We better get inside,' urged Grandpa Jock. 'There might
be satellites watching us.'

'And you lot have some catching up to do,' said Stan-Ley.

The alien had turned to Grandpa Jock, realising the
children were in need of an explanation, just as much as he
was in need of their help. Grandpa Jock opened the double
doors of his shed wide and gestured everyone inside to sit
on the sofa, the boxes and the two old stools in the corner.
They all sat, except the little grey creature.

'Are you going to tell them or shall I?' Grandpa Jock

started, pulling the shed doors closed behind him.

'Please, let me. I've been wanting to do this for years,' Stan-Ley began. 'Been telling my dad that you guys need to know this stuff but he keeps going on about the prime directive and non-contact and hands-off observation.'

'Well, it's catch up time.' Stan-Ley sighed and nodded, now ready to unveil the truth. 'We've been visiting your planet for nearly 100 years, since you started bombing each other and launching nuclear weapons. That's bad, man. I mean, bad for you, bad for your planet, bad for the galaxy. It's real dangerous too.'

Grandpa Jock raised one of his bony fingers. 'You see, I mentioned close encounters of the second kind before - evidence, you know - but we've skipped straight to the Third Kind - actual alien contact.'

'Some of us have been wanting to help you humans for years,' added Stan-Ley. 'To stop you guys blowing yourselves up and help with your world problems. But that non-contact rule just got in the way.'

'And that rule wasn't just an alien thing. Certain leaders here on earth wanted to keep the aliens a secret too. That's when I had my second meeting with your dad, back in the 1950's,' said Grandpa Jock, sharing history with the small group. 'Back when he met the American President, Eisenhower. The Greys just wanted to warn the world about the direction we were heading…'

'But oh noooooh…' groaned Stan-Ley. 'Some of your governments saw our arrival as a threat, and decided to shoot first and ask questions later. Now the United States military are preparing weapons in space that could get you dragged into an intergalactic war without you guys even having any warning.'

'And their alien technology could've eliminated the burning of fossil fuels within a generation…' added Grandpa Jock. 'We could've been saving our own planet years ago.'

'We wanted to help humanity but we couldn't welcome you into the galactic federation,' shrugged Stan-Ley, 'Because you lot are too war-like, and well, you're just not house-trained.'

'And most of the other aliens feel that way too,' sighed Grandpa Jock.

'Others? Most of the others?!' gasped Allison and Barbara at the same time. 'What others?'

'Yeah, we reckon that there's been at least four alien species visiting Earth for some time,' said Grandpa Jock, nodding his head towards the little alien, questioningly.

Stan-Ley just smiled. 'Sorry dude, I'm not supposed to say.'

'I know, it's a massive conspiracy. Our governments have been keeping quiet about this for years. I met with another species back in '57. They were called The Nordics,' said Grandpa Jock quietly. 'They were working with the government again, trying to stop us blowing ourselves up. But these higher alien civilisations actually banned Earth astronauts from venturing any further than the Moon until we "stopped killing each other" they said.'

Grandpa Jock went on. 'And their leader was a guy called Valiant Thor!'

"I stayed in and studied like a good little nerd. And fifteen years later, I'm one of the greatest minds of the 21st century."

Reed Richards, of the Fantastic Four.

Chapter 15 - Valiant Thor

Valiant Thor… what a cool name! And it's all true. Check it out online. Google it! Google Valiant Thor and see what it says. Some people have tried to hide the truth for too long. Some people think this stuff is too far-fetched to take seriously and some people might think you are just completely bonkers for believing in aliens…

But the truth is out there.

After the Roswell crash in 1947, the US government started to take serious interest in UFOs. That special group, Majestic 12, was set up to keep the whole project hush-hush and hundreds of flying saucers were seen across America in the next five years.

Then, on the evening of February 20th 1954, President Eisenhower went missing suddenly. Rumours circulated that he may have died, which prompted the official response that the president had gone to the dentist. They claimed he'd chipped his tooth.

In reality the president had been whisked off to an emergency meeting with an alien race said to be from the Pleiades star cluster. They are often referred to as The Nordics due to their pale blue eyes, blond hair, milky white skin and colourless lips.

The meeting took place at Edwards Air Force Base, in an empty hangar. The Nordics were worried about nuclear weapons, as those blasts were having a terrible effect on the fabric of space and time. They offered to share their superior technology, medical procedures and spiritual wisdom, as well as a replacement for fossil fuels with a clean energy source.

However, Eisenhower declined the ETs' offer because he did not want to give up his nukes. A deal was not reached and the meeting was abandoned.

Soon after, a second alien race made contact with Eisenhower and the leaders of the United States. Unlike the Nordics, the Greys managed to reach a deal with the president by suggesting that they would offer their new weapons to the Soviet Russia instead.

Worried that this would tip the balance of power in the Russians' favour, the president agreed to accept the advanced technology in return for access to members of the population. Essentially, the Greys had been given permission to abduct and experiment on citizens of the United States before wiping their memories and returning them unharmed.

Having agreed to allow their own citizens to be abducted by aliens, it is easy to understand why the US government wanted to keep quiet about the presence of extraterrestrials on our planet. Hence, the secrecy that still lasts until this day.

On 16th March 1957, Valiant Thor landed his spaceship, Victor One, in Virginia. He was greeted by two police officers, and using his telepathic powers, he arranged to be taken to the Pentagon to meet the US Secretary of Defense*.

*Stupid American spelling again!

Once Thor had convinced the Pentagon that he was from the planet Venus, he was ushered through a secret underground tunnel to the White House where he met with President Dwight D. Eisenhower and Vice President Richard Nixon.

The Victor One spacecraft was confiscated to be examined by scientists. Unfortunately, the best scientists on Earth had no understanding of electromagnetic rotary physics, gyroscopic energy propulsion, gravity waves, fibre optics or computer chips. They took decades to back-engineer this technology and are still working on many aspects of it today.

Although he looked human, Valiant Thor had six fingers on each hand. He also had an oversized heart, one very large lung, copper oxide blood, and an IQ estimated to be 1200. Plus, he spoke 100 languages, could walk through walls, and had a lifespan of 490 years.

According to Val (his preferred name), the Venusians had been sent to Earth by the High Council of Venus to protect Earth, and the intergalactic community, from its new nuclear capabilities, and subsequent nuclear warfare.

Sadly, the President told Thor that the offer to help Earth would destroy its economy. And the United States were simply not prepared to accept the Council's recommendations.

Surprisingly, after this refusal, Val was invited to stay behind and help American scientists better understand certain medical projects that would affect space science.

And he agreed! Thor was given living quarters in the Pentagon, his base of operations, for the next three years. During this time, he met with other world leaders and scientists, provided advice, and shared some technology.

After his tour of duty was up, Thor left Earth and returned to Venus on March 16, 1960. However, it is believed that Thor continued to assist Earth in surviving its tendency toward self destruction.

Perhaps NOW is the right time for Valiant Thor, or any other galactic diplomat, to return and make a public landing, and finally disclose the issue of intelligent life elsewhere in our galaxy.

Chapter 16 - Close Encounters of the Fourth Kind

Once Grandpa Jock had finished speaking, complete and utter silence filled the shed. Even Stan-Ley was amazed by the old Scotsman understanding of the ET presence on planet Earth. The alien blinked twice and Grandpa Jock turned towards him and nodded.

'Yeah, I heard it too.' A serious scowl had crossed his face, as his bushy eyebrows knotted together. This broke the spell that had engulfed the shed and all the children began to talk at once.

'You actually met aliens, Mr Jock?' asked Kenny.

'Do aliens still do experiments on humans?' gasped George

'Do the Greys still abduct people?' squealed Barbara, glancing over at Stan-Ley.

'Where's this guy Valiant Thor now?' asked Ben

'Do you still do experiments on cows?' hissed Allison

'Did you just read his mind, Mr Jock?'

'Are you telepathic, Stan?'

'What did you just say to him?'

'Who are the other alien species?'

'And where are they now?'

'**QUIET!**' snapped Grandpa Jock, and the kids stopped talking immediately. 'I think they're here.'

A low humming noise gently buzzed outside, slowly coming closer. A giant black shadow passed across the front of the shed window, and the bright sunlight shining in the window was replaced with an unearthly blue glow. The buzzing grew louder and the blue light seemed to electrify the whole shed. A box of tin cans in the corner began to shake. Tools on the walls started to vibrate. The ground shook and the kids gripped the arms of the sofa, or held onto the bottom on their stools. Stan-Ley was rooted to the spot. Only Grandpa Jock stood up.

No, he didn't just stand up. He was pulled up! Some powerful, magnetic force dragged Grandpa Jock against the wall of the shed and pinned him there, helplessly. The empty juice cans pressed into his wrinkly old skin and red welts started to appear on his arms and legs.

'Stan-Ley!' he cried. 'Get out of here!'

But before the small alien could move the shed doors slowly opened. What they all saw was beyond belief. Two people stood there... People? Were they people? Certainly neither male nor female but they were tall, with human-like features. Then they shimmered, phasing in and out of reality. One second people, the next second looking like lizards; nasty, green-skinned creatures.

The seconds they spent as people was becoming less and less, as if holding the human form took a tremendous amount of energy and concentration. Each relapse back to their reptile form came quicker and quicker... staying lizards for longer.

Still no one moved, until one of the Reptilians sprang forward to grab Stan-Ley, gripping his thin arms with its claws.

'Holy shizzle-sticks,' screeched Stan-Ley. 'He's got me!'

George and Ben were closest. They leapt to their feet, and jumped towards the large alien, yanking and tugging at its arms. It was too strong and the thing gripped Stan-Ley tighter.

The other giant reptile now stepped forward, hauling George and Ben away by their collars. The boys flew through the air, feet leaving the ground, backwards out of the shed door. The first Reptilian and the small Grey also disappeared out of the doorway and into the blue glow.

Seconds later, the brilliant beam of light vanished. The magnetic force-field that had pinned Grandpa Jock to the wall snapped off, and the old Scotsman dropped to the floor with a clanking clatter of tins and cans.

Barbara and Kenny dashed outside. Allison rushed over to the old geezer to help him up and Grandpa Jock slowly climbed onto his feet. Allison took his arm and they staggered out of the door.

The sun was shining again. There was no blue glow. There was no spaceship in the sky and the garden was empty. And there was no sign of George, Ben or the small grey alien known as Stan-Ley.

UNOFFICIAL–RECORDING

from Apollo 11 in July 1969:

"These "Babies" are huge, sir! Enormous!
OH MY GOD! You wouldn't believe it!
I'm telling you there are other spacecraft out there.
Lined up on the far side of the crater edge!
They're on the Moon watching us!"

Given to former NASA employee Otto Binder by unnamed radio hams. Recorded using VHF receiving facilities that bypassed NASA's broadcasting outlets.

Chapter 17 - Visitors

Grandpa Jock turned and walked slowly back into his shed. The tin cans clanked about his legs, as he pulled the metal sleeves from his iron suit. He snatched each one off with an angry tug and threw them into the box underneath his workbench.

He unpinned the metal chest plate with the torch and the Iron Brew emblem in the middle and dropped these into the box too. Then he began loosening the leg fastenings, as Allison, Barbara and Kenny shuffled into the shed.

'I'm sorry, kids,' he said sadly. 'It's my fault. I knew about the dangers when I saw that little alien but I just didn't think.'

'It's okay, Mr Jock,' replied Allison, putting her hand on his arm. 'Don't blame yourself.'

'Thanks Allison but it's still my fault. I've seen it before. I should've done more to protect you youngsters.' Grandpa Jock shook his head, as he threw his metal trousers beneath the workbench.

'Listen, Mr Jock,' spat Barbara. 'You can either sit there and feel sorry for yourself or you can get up off your bony old butt and do something about it. Those three are gone and they ain't coming back without our help.'

'That's right, Barbara,' shrugged the old Scotsman. 'They're gone. Abducted. Taken. Close encounters of the fourth kind... snatched by aliens. And unless we have a flying saucer, we are not getting them back.'

'What does this do?' asked Kenny, standing beside the workbench. He was picking his nose and pointing at the little red pebble sitting on the table.

'It's that stone you gave to Stan-Ley,' gasped Barbara.

'You said it was a calling card or something, wasn't it?' added Allison.

'Yeah, that Stan-Ley was impressed to see it. What does it do?' asked Barbara.

'That's a good question, Barbara.' Grandpa Jock's eyes were keen again, and his sparkle had returned.

'Hey! I asked that,' moaned Kenny but everyone ignored him, gathering around the smooth, dark red stone.

Grandpa Jock explained that he'd been given the pebble several decades ago by Stan-Ley's father, back when Grandpa Jock had worked for Secret Intelligence. Stan-Ley's father, who was known as Dorian, had presented the rock to Grandpa Jock when the Scotsman had saved the lives of several grey aliens during a fire-fight at the Dulce Air Force base. A squadron of Green Beret soldiers had stumbled upon a secret laboratory seven levels underground. The lab was filled with mutilated bodies of cows.

'The cows had died of natural causes,' added Grandpa Jock. 'The Greys were just doing experiments on the dead bodies. It was a misunderstanding.'

Back then, the shooting started immediately. Bullets and lasers zipped around the room, as the soldiers and the aliens fired on each other. There were a few casualties on both sides but Grandpa Jock escorted a group of Greys to safety before returning to calm the Green Berets. Dorian rewarded him for his role as peacekeeper.

'He gave me this pebble. The symbols carved onto one side of the rock are the lunar cycles from their binary star system.' Grandpa Jock picked up the small rock and held it gently between his thumb and forefinger.

'But what does it do, Mr Jock?' Allison was eager to find out.

'The rock has magnetic properties… gifts, if you like. Watch this.' And the old geezer reached into his box of empty tin cans and pulled one out. He stood the tin on the worktop and placed the pebble above the aluminium can. It floated just above the top of the tin, and almost immediately, the pebble began to spin around in circles, furiously. The can began to hum.

The noise wavered and warbled, notes rising and falling as the magnets inside the stone pulled the pebble in different directions. As the spinning continued faster and faster, the humming note grew higher and higher, until it was almost inaudible.

'I'd forgotten about this,' said Grandpa Jock. 'I've never had to use it before.'

'What's it doing,' asked Barbara, impatiently.

'It's sending out a signal, I think.'

'You think? Who do think it's sending a signal to?'

'Well, it's called the Commander's Calling Card, so I'm hoping the Commander will hear it.' Grandpa Jock added. 'Commander Dorian.'

'Stan-Ley's Dad?!' Kenny, Barbara and Allison all yelled at once but before Grandpa Jock could answer, there was a loud banging at the door.

'That was quick,' sniggered Kenny but Grandpa Jock just shook his head and put a finger up to his lips.

'Too quick,' he whispered and crept across to the door. He pulled the handle and the door swung outwards.

Standing outside were two huge men, easily over two metres tall. They both wore black overcoats, even though it was a scorcher of a day. Below their coats they had black suits with white shirts and black ties. Their black hats were pulled low across their faces, just above their dark sunglasses. Their collars were pulled up and they had serious, unsmiling expressions. Their lips were thin and straight.

'John Hansen?' asked one of the men, in a slow drone of a voice.

'Well, yes but everybody calls me Jock' replied Grandpa Jock.

'Mr Hansen,' the man went on. 'We have reason to believe that you may have been a witness to an unusual event recently.'

'No, no, not really,' stammered Grandpa Jock. 'Who are you guys anyway? Can I see some ID?'

'That will not be necessary, Mr Hansen. Just be aware that we are government agents and we ask the questions.' The man stared at Grandpa Jock, and Grandpa Jock stared back, blowing his moustache out.

'Down by the pond, on the other side of the trees?' asked the second man, in the same dull, monotone voice.

'No, I, erm, haven't left the house all day,' lied Grandpa Jock, raising his eyebrows and trying to look as innocent as possible. His eyebrows always popped up when he was telling even the whitest of little white lies.

'Are you sure, old man?' asked the first guy sternly.

'Positive,' squeaked Grandpa Jock. He'd just remembered that the pebble was spinning wildly on the workbench behind him.

One of the men in black tried to step beyond Grandpa Jock but the old fella blocked his way. The second agent stepped forward and Grandpa Jock hopped the other way to block him too but the first guy saw the gap and walked into the shed.

Barbara was sitting on the sofa with her feet up on a box. Allison was standing beside the workbench.

'What are you three doing here?' snapped the big man.

'We're just visiting Mr Jock,' answered Allison, rather too quickly.

'I live next door,' added Barbara, smiling. 'We've been here all morning… haven't left the place, have we?'

'What about you?' asked the agent, turning to Kenny, who was perched on the top of the workbench with his lips tight clenched.

'Just ignore him,' shrugged Allison. 'He never talks…'

'He's an idiot,' added Barbara.

'No, he's just mute,' said Grandpa Jock.

The agent stepped forward, removed his sunglasses and stared directly into Kenny's eyes; his face just inches away. Kenny's eyelids fluttered furiously

'Can you speak, son?'

Kenny kept his mouth closed and shook his head wildly. The agent stared at him for a few more seconds before turning to Grandpa Jock again.

'We will be watching you, old man.' And with that the two agents turned and walked out of the shed as quickly as they had arrived. Grandpa Jock looked at Kenny, turned towards Allison, then to Barbara, with his eyebrows raised, before asking,

'Where the heck is that pebble?'

Kenny let out a huge cough. The red rock shot out of his mouth and flew across the shed. He dribbled a little bit, and then spat on the floor.

'Urgh… tastes like dirt,' he hocked.

"The phenomenon of UFOs does exist, and it must be treated seriously."

Mikhail Gorbachov - Former President of the Soviet Union

Chapter 18 - Cell Smell

Inside the hangar, their cell was tiny, perhaps only eight paces long by six paces wide. There were thick metal bars around the sides and the ceiling was low. The floor was covered in straw. In the corner was an aluminium dog bowl filled with water. And the stench was horrific.

The cell to the left was empty, so too was the one to the right but directly opposite, and running the full length of the hangar, every single prison cell was crammed with cows... absolutely jam-packed with the beasts. They were a deep brown colour, none of them had horns and they all stood motionless and silent.

Every now and then, one of the animals would lift its tail and deposit another pile of steaming poo on the floor. The smell hung in the air, lingering. It was a deep, ugly smell of fear and flatulence that wrapped itself around every inch of space in the large hangar. Also hanging, this time high on the bars, were several harnesses, used to hoist the cows up.

George, Ben and Stan-Ley sat in their cell on the straw. They had been locked in there for exactly 2 hours and 37 minutes.

'Brown cows,' nodded George. 'Do you think they make chocolate milk?'

Stan-Ley's large black alien eyes rolled backwards but Ben just sniffed the air.

'Have you farted again, George?' asked Ben.

'No... I'm meant to be the Stink King,' groaned George. 'But it absolutely honks in here.'

'Okay dudes, enough already. That's the seventh time one of you has asked the other one if they've dropped a whopper,' moaned Stan-Ley. 'And every time we all know it's those poop machines over there.'

'So what is this place then?' asked George.

'And for the seventeenth time, I HAVE NO IDEA!' yelled Stan-Ley, losing his patience with the two lads. 'We've just been dumped in here, we've spoken to no one. I know as much as you do and...'

Stan-Ley stopped talking. There was a clank of metal on metal and a large door at the far end of the hangar opened slowly. Light from the corridor shone in from behind and three creatures with green scaly skin and sharp, yellow eyes walked across to the first cell. They slid open the gate and for the first time, George could make out a metallic sign above the doorway. It had strange markings printed across the front.

'Oh no,' whispered Stan-Ley. 'It's worse than I thought.'

One of the Reptilians placed its hand on the head of the first cow and guided it through the doorway. The cow shuffled its feet in a slow, plodding manner, as if hypnotised. None of the other animals in the cell moved, just kept staring down at their hooves, as the reptilian led the cow out through the hangar door. The other two aliens followed on behind without even a glance across at the boys' cell.

When the large metal door slid shut again, both George and Ben leapt on Stan-Ley, shouting wildly. The little alien backed away into the corner of the cell.

'What do you mean worse?' squealed George.

'Worse than what?' yelled Ben.

'It's maybe nothing,' replied Stan-Ley, holding out his open hands and trying to calm the two boys down.

'You know something,' said George, pointing his finger.

'We need to know what's happening here.' Ben looked quite determined, even if a little scared to hear the truth.

'Dudes... dudes... don't freak out on me now,' Stan-Ley said softly. 'It's just guesswork... I can't be certain.'

'**JUST TELL US!**' George and Ben shouted together.

Stan-Ley blew out a long blast of air from his thin mouth,

then drew in a deep breath. 'Okay, we know we've been taken by some Reptilians. This must be their ship. I've never been in one before but I've seen pictures.'

'The Reptilians are a nasty bunch, always fighting, always stealing stuff. Most of us other species just try to avoid them. That cow they took away is probably now being ripped apart, limb from limb. And they'll eat it raw.'

Both Ben and George puffed out their cheeks, as if to puke.

'But I saw that sign above the cell door… I can read it… I know what it means.'

'And?'

'I think it says LUNCH,' said Stan-Ley and both boys saw the little alien swallow hard. 'And there's a sign like that above our door too!'

'Shizzle-sticks!' groaned George and Ben together.

Chapter 19 - Your Planet Too - the really serious bit

What scares you, little reader? Snakes? Spiders? Zombies? What terrifies you so much that you might just poop your pants with a little less self-control? When your stomach churns and the butterflies in your belly are bursting to get out? When your knees actually knock and your feet are freezing?

I am scared of heights. Any higher than about two metres off the ground and I can feel myself seizing up. I hate those glass lifts in shopping centres. I hate high escalators... those really high ones in airports. I hate floor-to-ceiling windows at the top of tall buildings. I can't even get close to the edge of a high balcony and I feel physically sick when my wife pretends she is falling over said balcony (she's mean like that).

But recently, I have discovered a new fear. Climate change.

In 2018, the United Nation's Intergovernmental Panel on Climate Change (IPCC) warned that humans had only 12 years to save the Earth from a rise in temperature beyond 1.5°c. Even half a degree higher than this and the risk of drought, floods, wildfires, extreme heat and poverty would affect hundreds of millions of people.

These top scientists said that urgent and miraculous changes were needed to save the world from devastating changes.

The planet is currently 1.1°c warmer than pre-industrial levels. Climate change is already happening. We have had the warmest four years, between 2015 and 2018, since records began. We've had horrific hurricanes in the US, record droughts in South Africa and Australia, massive forest fires in California and even forest fires in the Arctic... yes, that's right... even forest fires in the Arctic! Every fraction of additional warming will worsen the impact, as the Earth seeks to balance itself.

Carbon dioxide levels in the atmosphere have risen by 15% in the last 25 years. Greenhouse gases are driving temperatures up to dangerous levels and global warming is accelerating.

Food scarcity and water shortages will soon be a huge problem and we will see a massive rise in heat-related deaths. We are already witnessing the extinction of tens of thousands of species. Insects, which are vital for pollination of crops, and plants are almost twice as likely to lose their habitat with a 2°c rise in temperatures.

This destruction of wildlife means that a sixth mass extinction in Earth's history is under way. And it's worse than previously feared. Scientists blame human overpopulation and overconsumption for the crisis. They warn that it threatens the survival of human civilisation, and we have just a short window of time in which to act.

Sea-level rises would affect billions of people with just a half-degree extra warming. Oceans are already suffering from an increase in acidity and lower levels of oxygen as a result of climate change. Sea ice-free summers in the Arctic will become the norm, unless we do something now.

So, climate change is scarier than vampires, more terrifying than your worst nightmares and marching towards us like a zombie apocalypse. Except… climate change is real.
And that's what really makes me poop my pants.

"We are the last generation
that can take steps to avoid
the worst impacts of climate
change. Future generations
will judge us harshly if we
fail to uphold our moral and
historical responsibilities."

Ban Ki-moon - Secretary General of the United Nations

Chapter 20 - Nick Poop Pops Up

Grandpa Jock jumped across his shed and picked up the red pebble. It was covered in Kenny's spittle, and the old Scotsman flicked a finger-full of drool from his hand.

Crayon Kenny was still picking bits of grit from out of his mouth and wiping his tongue on the sleeve of his pyjamas.

'Smart thinking, Kenny,' nodded Grandpa Jock. 'I'd forgot about the rock when those two goons banged on the door.'

'Don't thank me,' moaned Kenny. 'Barbara grabbed it and shoved it into my gob.'

'Who were these guys anyway, Mr Jock?' asked Allison, tilting her head to the side.

'The Men in Black... the real... men in black!' The voice came from the doorway of the shed, excited and stuttering in short bursts of words.

Everyone turned. Standing there was a tall, thin man in a navy suit and grey shirt. His hair was fluffy salt and pepper and he wore a pair of square-rimmed glasses. His face was serious but he had a mischievous twinkle in his eyes.

'Who the heck is this now?' cried Grandpa Jock, unused to visitors walking into his shed. And he'd had five children, one small alien, two large Reptilians, two big Men in Black and now one thin, grey man turn up in the last hour.

'Sorry... for barging in... like this. My name's Poop... Nick Poop.'

Grandpa Jock sniggered, Kenny burst out laughing, and even Allison managed to smirk.

'I am... a UFO investigator,' Nick Poop said with a straight face. 'I've been following those two... for days. What did they say to you?'

'Oh, just the usual,' grunted Grandpa Jock. 'We'll be watching you, be careful, all that sort of stuff. I know how to deal with those kinda guys.'

'Yes, Jock Hansen, isn't it?' babbled Nick Poop. 'I've read your file.'

'My... my file?' Grandpa Jock wrinkled his moustache.

'Oh yes... erm... I used to work for... the Ministry of Defence... in the UFO investigations dept... but now I'm what you'd call... freelance.'

'Whoa, whoa, whoa! You mean the government knows about aliens,' Barbara blurted out. 'And they're not telling anyone!' Her face was stern.

'Certainly,' nodded Nick Poop. 'They know a great deal more... than they care to admit. That's why I left... to get the truth out there.'

Nick Poop explained that he'd worked for the Ministry of Defence for twenty years, investigating UFO sightings to see if they were a threat to national security. Only, his evidence of aliens and flying saucers kept going missing from his desk overnight. Every time he found what he called a 'smoking gun', he would lock it away in his desk or his wall safe but it would be gone the following morning.

'I had an actual photograph... taken in Scotland... of a UFO and two military jets... but that was stolen too.'

People inside the government wanted to keep the knowledge of aliens top TOP secret, so Nick Poop resigned. And he had been investigating UFO sightings on his own ever since.

'I even managed... to use the Freedom of Information Act... to obtain American Government documents… about invisibility cloaking, wormholes between galaxies, gravity waves, warp drive, dark energy and even accessing extra dimensions in space.' Nick Poop's eyes sparkled as he spoke, revealing more and more top secret projects.

'That sounds like science fiction,' gasped George.

'More like science fact now,' nodded Barbara.

"Sounds like a great big pile of poop! You're POOP,' yelled Kenny, shaking his head. 'Our friends have been taken by a couple of lizard-men and we're sitting here talking about wormholes and warp drives.'

'Lizard-men… yes, that's how I arrived here…' he paused. 'I heard a message… on a secure radio channel… that an unidentified craft had been spotted… not far from here. By the time I arrived… the craft was gone… but the men in black had shown up. So I followed them to your shed. Did you see the spaceship? Did you see any lizard-men?'

Grandpa Jock held up his hand. 'Hold on, kids. Kenny's right.' Even Kenny looked surprised at that one. Grandpa Jock narrowed his eyes, suspiciously. 'Our only concern should be George, Ben and Stan-Ley… let's not talk about, er… anything else.'

'That's alright, Mr Hansen. I think the phrase you are looking for… is… "I can neither confirm nor deny the existence of aliens"… at least, that's what the official secrets act makes you say.'

Nick Poop continued. 'You see, most aliens have a prime directive… like Star Trek… never to interfere with a developing culture. To them, we humans are juveniles. The Greys say that we are already destroying our planet but the Reptilians will do it even quicker for us.'

'Reptilians?' Kenny butted in. 'Like those lizard-men?' Grandpa Jock put his finger up to his lips and Allison nudged Kenny in the ribs.

'Yes... but I believe the Greys want to step in and help us save the planet. Governments have had the ability to stop climate change for decades... but they don't want to... because it's all about money.'

'Because governments want us to keep burning coal and oil, and driving cars, and fighting wars, right?' Grandpa Jock gasped again, his whole worldwide conspiracy finally falling into place.

Nick Poop nodded sadly. 'Yes, and yet, all this time... billionaires are getting ready to abandon Earth and fly off to the bases on Mars.'

'Mars?' screeched Kenny. 'There are no bases on Mars!'

'Well, technically...' And as Nick Poop paused, Allison and Barbara jumped up excitedly.

'We knew it!' they squealed together, slapping high-fives to each other and fist pumping the air. 'We knew it! Don't you remember, Kenny? When we were doing that space project in school last year?'

'I never really remember much about school,' groaned Kenny but the girls continued.

'Barbara was studying that Space-X guy, Elon Musk,' Allison added.

'And Allison was looking at pictures from the Mars Rover,' Barbara continued.

'And Richard Branson, and Jeff Bezos from Amazon, and loads of billionaires were investing massively in space travel.'

'And the photos on Mars look like buildings.'

'So we reckoned that all the rich people were getting ready to abandon the Earth, whenever the planet was too toxic to live on.'

'But that old teacher Mrs McPherson told us we were being stupid!'

All the time the girls were talking Nick Poop just folded his arms and smiled. He nodded silently at the end of each sentence, as the girls' theory expanded. Finally, he said, 'And the truth shall set you free.'

'So,' added Grandpa Jock seriously. 'We keep spending, and consuming and practically giving our money to the richest billionaires in the world, who are using our cash to fund their escape plan.'

'You had better come with us, Jock. We have a lot of work to do.' said a strangely monotone voice from the doorway.

Grandpa Jock gasped again. There had been ZERO people, apart from his grandson, inside his shed in the last sixty years and already this morning he had eleven visitors, both invited and uninvited. The twelfth visitor was standing unseen, just inside the door.

Kenny thought; Stan-Ley was a small grey alien. Short, squat, with little arms and a large head. This visitor looked as if Stan-Ley had been put into a vice and stretched. It was tall, thin and the same pale grey colour. It had large black eyes and a thin mouth.

'**DORIAN!**' cried Grandpa Jock, his ginger moustache fluttering in surprise. 'You haven't changed a day! What have you been up to?'

The tall grey alien nodded. 'Later, Jock. First, we need to get our kids back!'

"People of good conscience need to break their ties with corporations financing the injustice of climate change."

The Most Reverend Archbishop Desmond Tutu - Human rights activist.

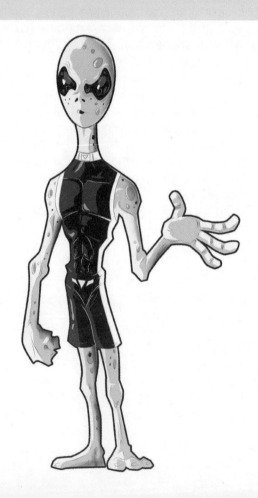

Chapter 21 - Sheeple

Superman once said "We're here to fight for truth, and justice, and the American way." We should add to that NOT!

Definitely NOT the American way! Consumerism - endlessly buying stuff - is killing our planet.

And it's not just America. The world's population are being kept just dumb enough never to question what's going on around them. Enough education to run the machines and fill in the paperwork but just stupid enough never to ask questions.

The REAL owners of the world are the big wealthy business people. The super-rich who make all the real decisions that affect all our lives every day.

They own us! They own you and me and everybody else on the planet.

26 men, (and they are all men because most women have real hearts) own more wealth than 3.5 billion people on this planet - yes, BILLION - more money than half of the world's population.

JK Rowling - that lovely lady who wrote those books about the wee wizard guy - Harry something or other - became a billionaire because her books were so popular but then she dropped out of billionaire status because she gave away so much of her money to good causes. Really, how much money do people need?

It's the greedy rich people who want more for themselves and less for everyone else.

You children, start asking questions, start demanding answers! Why is nobody doing anything? Who is profiting from this nonsense? Why do the ruling elite want to keep us in the dark?

Because they consider us Sheeple - not people, Sheeple! Blindly following whatever dumb nonsense they want us to believe in. Governments are a sham, to give the illusion of choice. The media, newspapers, radio, television and all the online internet giants are the bad guys. They are in on the trick, the sham, the scam... they all have their tickets on the one-way spaceships out of here, as soon as it's too toxic to live on our planet. We are the obedient workers who created that wealth for them - We are the Sheeple.

And they don't want us to come on their spaceships. They want to take everything we've got before they leave, stripping us and the whole planet bare, our wages and our pensions and your pocket money, and the water and the air and the crops and animals and wildlife, and then they'll be off - off to Mars or wherever.

It's a big rich man's club - and we ain't in it!

And they beat us over the head with that big club when they tell us what to think and what to buy. It's a fix, it's rigged and nobody seems to notice. Nobody seems to care because nobody shouts about it... BUT YOU! Young people, start shouting, raise your voices, make them heard and demand answers, and demand an equal share of the trillions that have been stolen from good, honest, hard-working people for centuries.

And that's what they count on, that we will always remain Sheeple. The owners of the world know the truth - and they don't want anyone else to hear it.

Chapter 22 - Lunch Is Served

'Have you just farted?'

'No,' sighed Stan-Ley. The two lads had been fart-joking for nearly two hours.

'Well, there's an awfully farty smell about here, and it's not coming from my bottom,' giggled George. Ben chuckled.

'Seriously, dudes… how long can you keep this up? I love a good fart joke just as much as the next Zetan but you two…' Stan-Ley stopped talking.

The large door at the far end of the hangar slammed open again. The boys looked across but none of the cows moved. Striding through the door were two huge reptilian creatures, stern-faced and eyelids blinking horizontally. They were very clearly lizard-men, they'd given up their human appearance as soon as the kidnapping was complete. They both had small, puckered-up little mouths, wrinkled like a dog's bottom.

'Dracos!' whispered Stan-Ley.

One was carrying a small box, whilst the other one held a large, gnawed bone in his right claw. The bone was almost stripped bare, flesh had been ripped off and what little meat that was still left was very obviously raw.

The Reptilians stopped outside the boys' cell and stared at each of them. Then, without moving their lips, they spoke. At least, the boys thought they spoke. Words appeared slowly in their heads, in English, with a slight accent and long drawn-out sss sounds.

We are only interesssted in the Grey.

You two were a sssurprise to usss.

The first Draco nodded across to George and Ben. The boys shifted back into the corner. The second lizard-man's puckered, little dog-bum mouth opened wide and he ripped at the raw meat on the bone again, pieces of flesh catching between its huge teeth.

'They're using telepathy,' gasped Ben. 'Speaking with their thoughts,' George nodded, his eyebrows darkening.

'Yeah, it's fairly common across the galaxy, guys. You should try it sometime… doesn't take long to learn,' Stan-Ley waved his hands around lazily.

You puny humansss are too primitive to communicate thisss way. Your brainsss are under-developed. We like your planet though. We ssshall enjoy usssing it.

'What do you want with us?' demanded George, jumping up. He stayed at the back of the cell though and hauled Ben up beside him.

Nothing hissed the alien without moving its mouth.
Only the Grey isss needed.

The reptilian carrying the box stepped up to the bars and pointed it towards Stan-Ley. The small Grey pulled his shoulders back and looked directly at the reptilian defiantly.

That will do. You will ssstay here for now.

'What about us?' yelled Ben, booting the bars of the cell. 'You can't leave us here.'

Ben kicked up straw and it fluttered gently around the cell. At one point, he knocked over the dog bowl in the corner, and water splashed across the floor. The Reptilians shuddered and the larger one stepped up to the bars of the cage.

You ssshould be grateful we have already eaten or you would be lunch. Ssstill, there'sss alwaysss tomorrow.

The Reptilians turned and walked toward the door again, leaving their three prisoners. Stan-Ley and George were carefully watching their captors, whilst Ben continued to take out his frustration by kicking the metal bars. Each kick was met with a loud clank, as the bars rattled in their frame.

Strangely, George noticed, each time Ben kicked the bars, the Reptilians ducked their heads a little, as if feeling the vibrations.

Chapter 23 - Calling Occupants

'It's been a long time, Jock.' The large Grey alien spoke as he walked along the decking of the space ship.

'Too long,' added the old Scotsman, pacing beside him.

'I only wish it could be in better circumstances,' Dorian replied.

At the end of the decking, two sliding doors slipped open, and Dorian stepped into a large conference room, followed closely by Grandpa Jock, Nick Poop, Barbara and Allison. Kenny trotted along behind them carrying a box of Iron Brew cans.

As they all entered the room, there were audible gasps and whispers. Outside the large bay windows lay a galaxy of stars that opened up beyond them. Below stretched out a massive blue planet. The Earth filled their view-screen, and not just with blues. The world was a myriad of colours; browns and green and yellows and a crown of white.

'May I present...' Dorian paused dramatically.

'... your planet.'

The tall alien stepped back and swept his arm majestically
across the viewing area. The five humans pressed closer for
a better view, until Kenny reached over too far and pushed
his face against the forcefield. A shimmer of electricity
rippled across the window and Kenny was zapped
backwards.

'I should have mentioned the forcefield,' said Dorian, smiling. 'Best not to touch it, Kenneth.' Crayon Kenny sat on the floor, rubbing his still-stinging nose.

Allison, Barbara and Grandpa Jock glanced at Kenny for a second then turned their heads back to the amazing view. Nick Poop didn't even bother looking towards the small boy;

he couldn't take his eyes off the panoramic scene.

Dorian the Grey explained that they were now travelling in a low Earth orbit, approximately 1,200 miles above the northern hemisphere. Below them lay the bright blue of the Atlantic Ocean, the less than whiteness of the Arctic and land masses of Europe on the right and Canada to the left. South America was at the bottom.

'What's that blue bit at the top?' asked Allison, pointing beyond the band of brilliant white.

Dorian raised his hands apologetically. 'That's the North Pole,' he said. 'It used to be covered in thick ice all year round but due to your global warming, it now melts during the summer months. The blue bit you see is the Arctic Ocean.'

'And what about that red-brown gash over here?' Barbara was pointing towards the left of the big window. 'It looks like a scar.'

'Yes, more bad news, I am afraid.' Dorian's head dropped onto his chest. 'That is what's left after the Greenland Glacier melted last summer. It has actually been melting four times faster than we first thought.'

'So why's that a bad thing?' muttered Kenny, pushing his way forward to the view screen.

'Well, as larger amounts of ice mass leave the glaciers as meltwater, they flow as rivers into the sea.' Dorian was speaking slowly and calmly, as if talking to an agitated child. 'For the last decade, Greenland had lost 280 billion tons of ice every year. That is enough to cover Florida, Texas and New York knee-deep in ice melt.'

Dorian continued, 'This is going to cause additional sea-level rise. The Greenland ice sheet is nearly two miles thick in places and if that melts, sea levels will rise seven metres. Global warming of just 1°c degree is causing that massive meltdown.

We are watching the ice sheet hit a tipping point right now.'

Everyone stared at the Earth. The devastation caused by deforestation was clear to see. Massive swathes of trees were being cut down throughout the Amazon and across the rainforest regions circling the globe... Indonesia, Africa, Brazil. Grey lines of polluted air ran across America and Europe and over every large city on the planet.

'So what can we do to stop the world heating up like that?' Barbara's eyes were wide and staring, as she suddenly realised that the Earth was changing dramatically.

'The whole world needs to cut carbon emissions now... massively. Stop burning fossil fuels, stop driving gas-guzzling cars, cut carbon emissions and invest in renewable energy. And most importantly, cut down on the amount of cow farts in your atmosphere.'

Everyone stopped and stared at Dorian. Grandpa Jock's eyebrow's popped up and Nick Poop turned away from the window, his jaw dropping open.

'Cow farts?' cried Kenny, delighted that someone was now talking his language. All that stuff about climate change and global warming had just gone right over his head before now.

Dorian smiled. 'It is true, Kenneth. Believe it or not, cow farts add an enormous amount of methane into the atmosphere. It's that methane and carbon that causes global warming. The more beef you humans eat, the more cows you need. The more cows you need, the more cows farts you have. The more cow farts you have, the warmer your atmosphere will get.'

The five humans slowly nodded, as if a giant energy-efficient light bulb appeared over their heads.

'The more cows you need, the more grazing land you use. The more grazing land you need, the more forests you burn down. The more forest you burn down, the more carbon is pumped into your atmosphere. You see, methane and carbon - absolute planet killers.'

'If we could only invent a machine,' Barbara was thinking furiously. '… that swallowed up all that carbon and methane, and even pumped clean air back into the atmosphere.'

'There are machines like that already,' laughed Dorian. 'They're called trees!'

Barbara slapped her hands together. 'Of course,' she cried. 'Cutting down trees is like ripping out our own lungs.'

'Yes, you are correct but right now, we have more urgent problems,' said Dorian.

'What?' cried Allison. 'More urgent that the end of the world?'

'Well, technically, if you humans keep going the way you are going, then we reckon you will destroy your world in about twenty or thirty years. It will be irreversible in ten.'

'Irreversible?' gasped Barbara.

'Yes, no going back,' shrugged the large Grey. 'But if we

do not stop the Dracos now, then they will destroy your planet in about six months. Strip it clean… kill, eat and ravage everything and everyone. Come this way.'

Dorian gestured over the little pod-chairs on the other side of the room. They all sat down, arranged in a semi-circle around a flat, black panel on the wall. Dorian placed three fingers on the panel and a screen lit up. A picture of a lizard-man appeared.

'Draco spies have been visiting Earth for several decades, using their shape-shifting as a disguise,' Dorian began.

While they had been repairing their space ships on the dark side of the moon, Dorian explained, the Reptilians had been visiting Earth, stealing cows and abducting humans, to experiment on them. They were testing for human weaknesses. They even signed a secret treaty with most of the world's governments to allow experiments on humans, in exchange for advanced technology.

'Do not talk to strangers, kids,' urged Dorian. 'These aliens farm children for pure energy in secret bases in New Mexico.'

'So… flying saucers and alien abductions… are real!' Nick Poop had just jumped up from his pod-seat. He had been silent ever since being beamed onto the Grey's spaceship, amazed by the technology, and trying to absorb everything he saw. This was everything he had lived his life to prove.

'Yes, Mr Poop, it is all true,' agreed Dorian. 'We Greys, along with a few other species, have been visiting your planet for centuries, quietly. We consider Earth to be a human zoo. We watch you but we do not like to interfere.'

'And everything our ancestors witnessed… flying carpets, dragons, sky-gods… they were all real too.' Nick Poop paused again. 'We just dismissed them… as folk-tales… and magic.'

'What your ancestors thought was magic…' Dorian said softly. '…We call science. It was really just misunderstood technology. As a species, the Greys are about quarter of a million years ahead of you humans.'

'We were right all along,' gasped Nick Poop. 'People thought we were mad to believe in Ancient Aliens... but we only need to be proved right once. Sceptics and non-believers need to be right... every time... again and again but all we needed was one little bit of proof... of alien life somewhere in the universe... and we were right.'

'And that is where your obsession with superheroes started,' said Dorian, pointing to Kenny's costume. 'From the beginning of recorded history, humans have told stories about beings with super-human strength, super-sonic speed, and supernatural abilities. Your people thought these were just myths and legends but there was an otherworldly reason... Superheroes were actually based on extraterrestrials in the distant past.'

'Of course,' cried Kenny. 'Why didn't I see it before! Superman was an alien from the planet Krypton. Thor was an alien. Wonder Woman was an alien. Dr Who and the Autobots and the Saiyans from Dragonball Z... all aliens! Venom and the Silver Surfer, even Captain Marvel was transformed by ALIENS!!'

Kenny's rant was interrupted by a bleep from the wall panel. Dorian touched the glowing green light with one of his fingers and said 'Go ahead.'

A voice replied, 'Sir, we have an incoming transmission from the Draco ship.'

'Put it on audio.'

Silence swept across the control room. A picture of Stan-Ley appeared on the screen, behind bars but looking defiant. Static crackled through the speaker and a slow rasping whisper began...

"It isss our intention to take the Earth. Do nothing. Do not interfere. We have your sssson. You have been warned."

Chapter 24 - Of Interplanetary Craft

In the control room, no one spoke. Dorian stood perfectly still, with his head cocked slightly to the side. Grandpa Jock's moustache rippled up and down as he pressed his lips together tightly, deep in thought. Kenny and Allison exchanged fearful glances but Barbara had wandered off towards the large bay window again.

Suddenly, the control room door swished open and another tall Grey appeared, walking quickly. The alien wore a shiny, black outfit, high at the neck and sleek around the body.

'Cool suit,' whispered Barbara.

'Commander. The reptilian ship is closing in. It will be passing directly overhead in six minutes.'

Grandpa Jock laughed coldly. 'We used to say "there's a bogie at twelve o'clock."'

Instinctively, Kenny thrust a finger up to his nose and fiddled about with each nostril, clearing any debris that might have been lingering. Then he looked at his watch and realised that it was already two in the afternoon.

'This situation is serious, Jock,' nodded the commander, as he touched the black screen in front of him. 'But you know our policy... complete non-intervention. We just cannot interfere with your culture.'

'But they've got your lad,' grunted Grandpa Jock. 'And George and Ben. If you won't get them back, then I will.'

'How do you plan to do that?'

'I huvnae worked that bit oot yet,' spat Grandpa Jock, his accent more guttural with the urgency of the moment. 'Even if I have to fly doon there and get them myself.' and he winked across to the girls, his eyes sparkling.

'Dorian, dude,' interrupted Barbara, as she turned towards the commander. 'Look, any chance I can wear one of those suits, like that guy. I'm still wearing fluffy pyjamas here, man, and my dad's old t-shirt. It's way too big for me. If I'd known I was coming on board a flying saucer I would've...'

'Alright, alright,' snapped Dorian. 'Take the children to central storage. Feed them, cloth them, anything. Just keep them safe and out of the way.'

Before the Grey could escort them out of the control room, Allison stepped towards the old Scotsman.

'Are we in danger, Mr Jock? Dorian said it was serious.' Allison had a worried expression across her face.

'It'll be fine, young lady. Don't you worry.' said Grandpa Jock, shaking his head. His eyebrows were now popping upwards to meet his long-gone hairline and Allison looked at him suspiciously.

'Let me tell you about the Battle of Los Angeles,' he began. 'In 1942, a huge UFO appeared in the skies above southern California and was picked up by dozens of spotlights. The Americans had just been dragged into World War Two, so the Yanks naturally thought the aircraft was Japanese. It wasn't... it was actually this spaceship here. And they fired 1,400 missiles at this craft and no damage was done. Nothing. Zip, zilch, nada. Not one missile put a scratch on this baby. There's a forcefield all around this ship. So, you're probably in the safest place on Earth... or above Earth anyway.'

Allison glanced across to Dorian. The commander had dropped his head and shuffled sheepishly. He shrugged and nodded but said nothing. The other Grey held his hand out and ushered the children through the door with three open fingers, and they all filed out.

'You did not talk of the Reptilians' lasers, Jock,' whispered Dorian. 'Missiles might bounce off our forcefield but those lasers could blast us out of the sky.'

'Maybe best we didn't mention that, eh?' nodded Grandpa Jock, grimly.

Allison and Barbara marched quickly alongside the large Grey, whilst Kenny trotted along behind them carrying the box of tin cans again. Barbara had nodded towards the box as they left the control room and had fixed Kenny with a steely glare. He knew he had no choice but to bring it along.

Allison nudged Barbara and opened her eyes wide, as if to ask her a question. Barbara shrugged and shook her head, not sure of the answer. Kenny just huffed and puffed at the back.

They turned along a corridor and the doors at the end swished open. Inside was a small store room, no bigger than a walk-in wardrobe. It was filled with rotating shelving units, sealed inside clear plastic boxes. The Grey flicked at the strange symbols on the wall panel and one of the plastic boxes popped open. He pulled out a stiff, black outfit similar to his own, only smaller. The material was definitely black but it seemed to shimmer in the light. He handed it to Barbara and she took it. It was much lighter than she expected.

'We call the material vibranium but you know it as Kevlar.' The Grey turned and walked out of the store room.

'Kevlar!' hissed Kenny. 'Wow, that stuff can stop bullets.'

'This is probably where Kevlar comes from, originally… like a gift from the Greys,' said Allison.

KZZZKT!

'Mr Jock did say that science was given a boost when the aliens made first contact fifty or sixty years ago,' added Barbara, not looking directly at them. She was too busy pushing buttons, popping open boxes and pulling out the contents.

'Are you thinking what I'm thinking?' asked Allison, her eyes beginning to light up.

'You saw Mr Jock's face.' Barbara smiled and she winked at Allison. 'He wants us to do this!'

It was at that moment that a loud explosion erupted above their heads, the whole room shook, then they were plunged into darkness.

The lights had gone off in the control room too, and only the blue glow from the Earth below shone in, casting long shadows across the ceiling. Grandpa Jock ran to the viewing window and gasped as a huge black spaceship sailed over their heads.

'That was just a warning shot,' gasped Dorian, as the light from Earth began to be blocked out by the massive vessel above them. It was a dark, triangular shape with single lights in each corner. Occasionally, lights flickered on and off around the edges of the ship, until eventually the Greys' saucer had been completely overtaken.

Ahead, the tip of the triangle and the fringes of the enormous spacecraft began to glow orange, as the ship entered the Earth's atmosphere. Dorian was furiously sliding his fingers across the black panel on the table in the middle of the room. Grandpa Jock saw that there were no buttons, switches or dials on the surface… it was all just touch-screen.

'We must go in after them!' shouted Grandpa Jock, and as soon as the words left his mouth, the saucer ship glided forward. There was no bump or jolt, just a smooth increase in speed and the viewing window began to shimmer with an orange flicker. The blackness of space melted into a deep blue of the upper atmosphere and finally, the bright azure of a summer's day lit up the control room.

'Engage the cloaking device,' shouted Dorian into the microphone on the desk and the viewing window shimmered again. Grandpa Jock glanced across to his right and saw Nick Poop, sitting still and quiet, at the end of the row of pod chairs. His face was paler than before and his hair looked greyer. His hands were cupped around his mouth and he was whispering under his breath.

Grandpa Jock shouted across. 'Are you alright there, Mr Poop?'

'It was all true,' he said quietly. 'Los Angeles, Roswell, Betty and Barney Hill, Kecksburg, Rendelsham Forest… it's all true.'

'Yeah, it hit me pretty hard too, first time.' Grandpa Jock's shoulders jiggled as he spoke. 'When your knowledge of the old world stops dead, then your understanding of the future starts here.'

'Do not worry about him,' shrugged Dorian. 'This happens a lot. He will be okay once his brain comes to terms with the new reality.'

'Mr Poop?' Grandpa Jock called over. 'Nick? They had to stay under the radar, Nick. We shot at them. We did experiments on them. We treated them really badly, so how would you behave? The aliens went totally hands off!'

'Well, not entirely,' Dorian added. 'Some alien species still want to exterminate the human race. They consider you vermin.'

"Of course flying saucers are real, and they are interplanetary."

Lord Dowding GCB, GCVO, CMG*-
Air Chief Marshal in British Royal Air Force.
Air Command Officer RAF Fighter Command

Chapter 25 - Your Planet Three
- The really *really* serious bit

*Right, little reader, here is a bit of the serious stuff now.
I don't mean to alarm you but I really think you need to
know this...*

*Our planet is in trouble! And when I say 'our' planet, I
actually mean 'yours', or what will be left of it. And it's not
even your fault.*

*You see, my generation, and the two generations before
that, have really messed up the world for everybody. Us
old people have known about global warming and climate
change for decades but we've done next to nothing about
it. And I'm really, really sorry about that.*

*Some people are still denying there's a problem so this is
why I'm telling you stuff now.*

*Governments have done nothing about it because it would
cost them votes. Big businesses have done nothing about it
because it would cost them profits. Most people just want
to sweep the whole mess under the carpet and it's your
generation, the youngest people on the planet, who are
going to pay the price. Us oldies are gonna be dead soon
enough but you will need to deal with the world after that.*

*The world is a living, breathing organism - it's alive and it
needs clean air and fresh water and a healthy eco-system to
keep that balance. And without that, then the planet will be
unable to sustain life as we know it.*

*Imagine that all you ever eat is fast food, sugary snacks
and fizzy juice. Pretty soon you would be an enormous blob
of fat, wobbling around with no energy and your brain would
be turning to mush. And I would blame your parents, or
whoever looks after you, for not giving you a healthy diet.
Grown-ups who should know better.*

Well, the grown-ups on Earth should've known better

*about caring for the Earth but they've been forcing a diet
of plastic and pollution and fossil fuels into the planet for
decades, thinking they knew best.*

*They've been chopping down trees and digging up land
and burning all mess of chemicals into the atmosphere and
the world is choking on this filth.*

*And at some point the Earth is gonna say 'ENOUGH'.
It's gonna go on a crash diet, and it's gonna detox and
it's not gonna be pretty.*

*Global Warming is a bad phrase. The world is not just
going to get warm. It's not just gonna be like a summer's
day at the beach, and even that idiot President with the
stupid hair doesn't get it. Some parts of the world are going
to boil and other parts are going to freeze. It's not just
climate change, it's a climate crisis!*

*Parts of the world will flood with record rainfall, whilst
other parts will experience droughts for decades. Ice
caps are already melting. Sea levels are already rising
and weather will get weirder. We are already causing
the extinction of tens of thousands of living species
across continents.*

*And you know what? People will say this is the end of the
world but it's not... the world will survive. It's just people,
plants and animals that will die off... maybe even all of us.
It's happened before, look at the dinosaurs... the world
carried on. It changed a bit but the big blue planet was still
the third rock from the Sun. Only, life had to change to fit
around the world's rules.*

*And we, the old people, did this. The grown-ups who
are meant to know better stuck their heads in the sand
and ignored the problems. We should've changed our way
of life, we should've done something about it, instead of
being caught up in our world of shopping and eating and
television and buying new stuff all the time.*

Even if some people didn't buy into those commercials, we still said nothing or did nothing to change it.

You, little reader, can change this. You need to change it. You need to help everyone on the planet realise that they need to change too. Shout loud. Shout louder. Make your voice heard because you know what needs to be done.

It's gonna be your planet soon enough…. technically, it's already yours. But the old people will hand it over to you and it's gonna be in a real mess. Well, start shouting now, and tell them to fix it before it's too late.

"We are in a planetary emergency!"

Prof. James Hansen, former Director - NASA Goddard Institute for Space Studies

Chapter 26 - Sound Affects

The boys had been sitting in silence for over an hour, still wrapped in the warmth of bovine bottom burps but even George was tired of the same old jokes. At one point, Ben suggested that the room was heating up but Stan-Ley knew that the Reptilians' spaceship was only entering the Earth's atmosphere. Once the ship levelled out, the room became cooler again.

'Do they really want to eat us?' groaned George, almost resigned to his fate.

'Yes, I'm afraid so, man. The Dracos will eat anything,' replied Stan-Ley. 'And this lot seem particularly nasty.'

'But what do they want with you, Stan?' Ben thumped one fist into his open palm. 'What good is a little grey alien to these psychos?'

'I've been thinking about that too,' said Stan-Ley. 'Trying to piece this whole thing together. Listen...'

And Stan-Ley explained his theory. It all began thousands of years ago, when various alien species began visiting the Earth. Humans were an interesting project to observe but now and again, the aliens would let their guard down and people would see a spaceship. This led to humans thinking that the aliens were Gods and that's how religions started.

After that, most aliens backed off, to let the people of the world develop naturally. The intergalactic Council of Planets tasked the Greys with the role as Watchers.

But when World War One, then World War Two broke out, the aliens became deeply worried by the humans' hostility towards each other. They had always been an aggressive species but these conflicts took the problem to a whole new level. The invention of the atom bomb was the final straw.

Shortly after the detonation of the nuclear bombs over

Hiroshima and Nagasaki, the Roswell Air Force Base was the only nuclear armed squadron base in the world. An increase in UFO activity was reported in the area because the aliens had increased their activity - obviously - worried about the fact that humans have in-built ability to destroy themselves. Then two spacecrafts collided. Alien bodies were recovered in the wreckage and governments became even more secretive.

Around this time, the Reptilians landed their spaceships on the dark side of the moon. They were exhausted by their travels across several galaxies and took time to rebuild their civilisation, not that they were very civil. Secretly visiting Earth, the lizard-men studied and stole from humans, making false deals with governments and preparing for the day that they could take over the world.

And that day had finally arrived.

The Reptilians knew that the humans were destroying their world. The Greys knew that the humans were destroying their world. Even the humans knew that humans were destroying their own planet but nobody was doing anything to stop it. The Reptilians had to move in, whilst there was still something left to steal.

And by tracking, then snatching Stan-Ley... the Dracos hoped to control the Greys, and allow the Reptilians to take control of the Earth without interference.

'And that's why we're here,' announced Stan-Ley. 'At least, that's why I'm here. I'm a hostage. You two arrived by accident.'

'Accident, my butt!' yelled Ben. 'Those lizards took us... they knew they were taking us... because we were trying to save you. And now we're stuck here... and those freaks are going to eat us for breakfast!'

Ben kicked the cage again and the bars rang like a gong, echoing around the huge hangar. Two or three cows mooed their objections and three or four of them farted in response. One large cow lifted its tail and dropped an enormous pile of poo onto the floor.

George jumped to his feet. 'Let's not start fighting amongst ourselves. We're in this together and nobody is to blame, except the lizards. Now Stan-Ley, tell me the part about the dark side of the moon again.'

The little mental cogs inside George's brain were whirring round furiously as Stan-Ley explained about the Dracos landing on the far side of the lunar surface, and their life in the silence of space. Ben started to nod too, once George revealed his plan.

'I saw them shudder earlier, when you were kicking the bars, Ben,' said George, getting excited. 'And Stan, you reckon their ears are not used to noise.'

'Space is a vacuum, dude. Sound doesn't travel well,' agreed Stan-Ley. 'And they would want to stay quiet, to avoid being picked up by radars and satellites.'

'So a loud banging noise would be a shock to their system,' laughed George.

'Let's put it to the test,' grinned Ben, picking up the water bowl that was lying empty in the corner.

"I am convinced that UFOs exist because I have seen one."

President Jimmy Carter - 39th President of the United States of America

Chapter 27 - Vermin

'Vermin?' shouted Grandpa Jock, upset by Dorian's last comment. 'It's you guys who abandoned little Stan in the woods. And you refuse to go back to save him. He's your son!'

'I am truly sorry, Jock but our prime directive is non-contact with primitive species,' nodded Dorian. 'He may be young by our standards but he is close to one hundred years old by yours. Stan-Ley understands this.'

'Primitive?' Grandpa Jock was yelling again. 'We put men on the moon!'

'Yes, and the Reptilians told you never to return,' sighed Dorian, losing patience with the old Scotsman. 'That is why you humans have never been back to the moon in almost 50 years.'

'Reptilians don't scare me,' screamed the old geezer. 'At least I have the nerve to save those boys! You're too arrogant to even try.'

'Let me tell you about arrogance, Jock.' said Dorian softly. 'First, your people thought that the Earth was flat... clearly we know it is not.' He calmly walked across to the view-screen and spread his hand out across the crescent of the blue horizon.

'Then you thought your planet was the centre of the Universe - it is most definitely not. That the Sun revolves around the Earth? It does not. The Church used to torture and kill anyone who disagreed with their ideas.'

Grandpa Jock stopped and stared at Dorian. Maybe it was just his moustache quivering but then again, perhaps it was his bottom lip. His eyes were glassy and twinkled like stars in the sky.

'You live on an insignificant little planet on the edge of an island of stars in a small galaxy called the Milky Way,'

Dorian continued. 'Technically, it is a spiral galaxy, with two spinning arms around a central belt of stars. You are located on the smaller arm, more than 25,000 light years from the centre of your galaxy. You may know it as Orion's Spur.'

Dorian sighed again. 'And still some humans believe that you are the only intelligent species in the galaxy, when you are surrounded by 10 billion other planets. How arrogant is that!'

'But we didn't know any better,' argued Grandpa Jock.

'Ignorance is no excuse, Jock. Some alien species consider you humans vermin because you are killing your own planet.' Dorian spoke calmly, emotionless and cold. 'You are like frogs in a pot of water. The pot is slowly boiling so you do not jump out. But you will still boil.'

'Okay, I admit, we are facing our extinction... either by these Reptilians or by climate change. But still, you'll do nothing to help us?' Grandpa Jock asked, the steely determination in voice returning.

'We are just the Watchers, Jock,' said Dorian softly. 'Inter-stellar civilisations are graded on how advanced and enlightened they are, from level one up to three hundred. Earth is scored zero because you keep killing each other.'

Grandpa Jock growled. 'Right, then I'll do it myself then. Maybe one person can make a difference.'

'The greatest threat to your planet is the belief someone else will save it,' nodded Dorian the Grey. 'Act now... save the planet and your future.'

"Act now to save our planet and our future from the climate emergency."

Antonio Guterres, UN Secretary-General

Chapter 28 - Your Planet Four -
The *really* REALLY *really* serious bit!

So serious in fact that mums and dads and teachers might not like this bit but I think it needs to be said… in a serious voice. You could skip this chapter but that would be a shame. <clears throat> AHEM!

This is our darkest hour.

Humanity is caught up in an event never seen before in its history. One which will catapult us into the destruction of the planet, unless we can fix it. Every nation, every person on Earth, our ecosystems and future generations will be affected.

The science is clear. There is almost total agreement among climate scientists and organisations that human beings have caused a dramatic increase in the amount of carbon dioxide and methane released into Earth's atmosphere. This is driving the climate catastrophe.

We are in the planet's sixth Mass Extinction Event and we will face catastrophe if we do not act swiftly.

Biodiversity is being wiped out around the world. Our seas are poisoned, acidic and rising. Our air is toxic. The breakdown of our climate has begun. Food supplies and fresh water will disappear and 97% of 10,000 climate scientists agree that this is happening.

This eco-crisis can no longer be ignored.

In 2018, the United Nation's IPCC warned that humans had only 12 years to save the Earth and since then, governments have done nothing.

The idiots in charge of the world chose to ignore this report, like that stupid, orange lunatic in America, with the tiny hands and the even smaller brain, who doesn't even believe in global warming… burning more and more coal and oil and selling off the gas reserves around the American coast, drilling for shale gas with a process called fracking, undermining the surface of the planet, polluting water and causing sink holes to appear that swallow up people houses.

<And breath>

The world used to have proper statesmen - true leaders - like Lincoln, Roosevelt, Mandela, Kennedy, Churchill and Obama. But now America have a circus for a government with a clown as president in charge of the world.

And the trouble with stupid people, even presidents, is that they are too stupid to know how stupid they really are!

All the bickering and squabbling just diverts the public's attention away from the true challenges and dangers facing the world.

I don't say all this to scare you, little reader. You are smarter than that. I just think you should know about this, so you can do something about it. In order to find the solutions needed to avert this catastrophe and to protect the future, it becomes your right and your sacred duty to rebel.

A young student in Sweden, Greta Thunberg, then aged 15, went on strike, refusing to go to school until the government listened to her calls to tackle climate change. Her protests captured the imagination of a country that has been struck by heatwaves and wildfires in its hottest summer since records began 262 years ago. Sweden enacted the most ambitious climate

law in the world, aiming to become carbon neutral by 2045.

"This is too little too late, it needs to come much faster,"
Thunberg said.

But she did not do this alone. Some teachers joined her
in the protest, even expecting to lose wages and even their
jobs. One said,

"Greta is a troublemaker, she is not listening to adults.
But we are heading full speed for a catastrophe, and in this
situation the only reasonable thing is to be unreasonable."

And Greta's solitary protest outside the Swedish
Parliament in Stockholm has sparked off a global movement
called Fridays For Future. Now school children are
protesting about climate change in front of their council
building or town hall every Friday. Pupils hold up banners
and signs with #FridaysForFuture and #ClimateStrike.

Of course, school children are required to attend school.
But with the worsening Climate Destruction, going to
school begins to look pointless. Why study for a future
which may not be there? Why spend time and effort
becoming educated, when governments do not listen
to the educated?

Since Greta's protest began, tens of thousands of pupils
in cities across Europe and as far away as Australia,
Uganda, Mexico and the United States have walked out
of their Friday classes to push for more ambitious carbon-
cutting targets.

Greta has even taken her message to world leaders
directly, at an EU conference in Strasbourg. There,
she urged governments to double their efforts to cut
greenhouse gas emissions.

"Everyone believes that we can solve the crisis without
effort, without sacrifice. We can't!"

In March 2019, Greta Thunberg, the founder of the
Youth Strike for Climate movement, was nominated
for the Nobel Peace Prize.

> "Why bother to learn anything in school if politicians won't pay attention to the facts? What am I going to learn in school? Facts don't matter any more, if politicians aren't listening to the scientists, so why should I learn?"

Greta Thunberg - Teenage Climate Change Activist

Chapter 29 - Suits You, Sir

Just as Dorian said 'Act now... save the planet and your future' the door to the control room swished open with a whoosh and a flurry of children burst through. Even Nick Poop looked up from his dream-come-true. The truth was finally beginning to dawn on him.

Barbara led the way, wearing the same tight Kevlar suit the aliens wore. She looked lean and strong... powerful even. Her jet-black hair was pulled back off her face and she wore an expression of grim determination.

Allison was just a pace behind her. She still wore her pink leggings but now she had Barbara's dad's red t-shirt on. She had a strip of Kevlar pulled tightly around her waist and this made the huge t-shirt look like a skirt. Another strip of Kevlar had been cut into a mask across her face. She looked ready for action too.

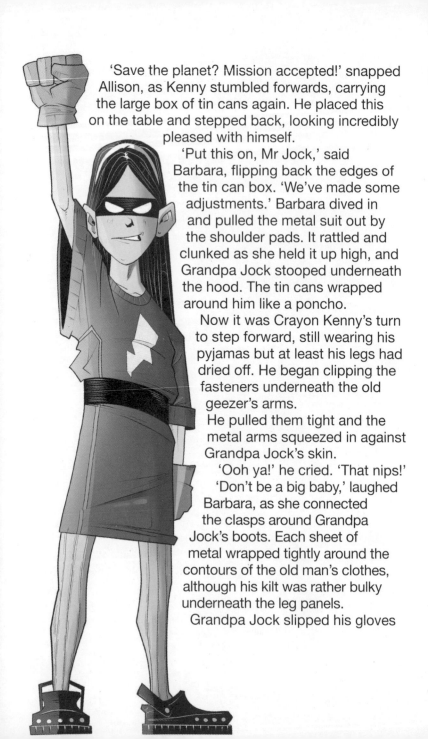

'Save the planet? Mission accepted!' snapped Allison, as Kenny stumbled forwards, carrying the large box of tin cans again. He placed this on the table and stepped back, looking incredibly pleased with himself.

'Put this on, Mr Jock,' said Barbara, flipping back the edges of the tin can box. 'We've made some adjustments.' Barbara dived in and pulled the metal suit out by the shoulder pads. It rattled and clunked as she held it up high, and Grandpa Jock stooped underneath the hood. The tin cans wrapped around him like a poncho.

Now it was Crayon Kenny's turn to step forward, still wearing his pyjamas but at least his legs had dried off. He began clipping the fasteners underneath the old geezer's arms.

He pulled them tight and the metal arms squeezed in against Grandpa Jock's skin.

'Ooh ya!' he cried. 'That nips!'

'Don't be a big baby,' laughed Barbara, as she connected the clasps around Grandpa Jock's boots. Each sheet of metal wrapped tightly around the contours of the old man's clothes, although his kilt was rather bulky underneath the leg panels.

Grandpa Jock slipped his gloves

on and lifted his arms up like a starfish. Sturdy black mesh spread out beneath his arms. It was glued to both sides of his body and down the length of his legs.

'I look like a giant bat,' he squealed, stumbling.

Kevlar material had been glued onto his leg irons and formed a tight, triangular wedge between his feet.

'More like a flying squirrel, Mr Jock,' giggled Kenny, grabbing onto the old man's arm to support him.

'You might need to shuffle, Mr Jock. We made you a Wing-Suit for flying in… but it's a bit tricky to walk in,' added Barbara.

'It was Barbara's idea,' said Allison, nodding across to her friend. 'She's full of great inventions. We cut up one of their space suits.'

'I've seen it on the telly, Mr Jock,' Barbara continued. 'There's a sport called BASE Jumping. This suit will help you glide…' she paused. 'And I thought you wanted to get across to the Reptilians ship.'

'Aye,' moaned Grandpa Jock. 'But I wanted a shuttle craft or a helicopter or something. I wisnae planning to jump!' Grandpa Jock's Scottish dialect was becoming stronger again.

'You'll be fine, Mr Jock.' Allison was trying to sound reassuring. 'It was Barbara's idea.'

'You'll be fine,' said Barbara. 'The suit is structurally sound, the wings are Kevlar. It's strong and it's aerodynamic and Kenny says you've done some parachuting in your younger days.'

'Aye but that was fifty years ago!'

'Well, we've fitted a mask for you,' added Allison, sliding a face-plate over the old fella's baldy head. It looked like a diver's mask.

'And we've added a set of headphones too,' Barbara went on. 'So we can talk to you when you're flying.'

Dorian slipped the huge set of headphones over Grandpa Jock's ears. He flicked a switch on the battery back around Grandpa Jock's waist and a glowing light appeared on his chest.

'Whit's this noo!' squealed Grandpa Jock.

'That's a loudspeaker and your torch, Mr Jock,' smirked Kenny. 'Just in case you need to yell for help or attract attention. And it's attached to your i-Pod. That was my idea.'

'Oh aye… and whose idea was it to put me into the iron suit before I went to the toilet,' he groaned. 'I'm no' as young as I used to be, you know.'

Kenny gulped. 'You need to go to the toilet? Like, right now? How do you go to the bathroom in an iron suit?'

There was a long pause, and Grandpa Jock stared at the ceiling casually, whistling softly under breath. A small puddle appeared at his feet.

'Just like that,' he chuckled, and gingerly shook one of his legs, which rattled and dripped.

'Aw man, I hope your suit doesn't go rusty now,' said Kenny, carefully stepping clear of the puddle of wee.

"You know, sometimes when you cage the beast, the beast gets angry."

Wolverine, X-Men: The Last Stand

Chapter 30 - Shake, Rattle and Hole

'Buttheads!' shouted George.

'Buttheads!' yelled Stan-Ley.

'Buttheads!' screamed Ben at the top of his lungs.

'And again… Buttheads!' shouted George, and the cows bellowed their disapproval once more. Stan-Ley and Ben joined in, getting louder again.

The boys had been shouting continually for ten minutes and the animals in the cages opposite were becoming more and more upset. They had grown used to the almost-perfect silence onboard the spaceship and were not enjoying the sudden, and noisy, interruption.

There was no room in their cage to stampede but most of the cows were now staggering and shuffling back and forth. Their hooves would thump down on the metal panels on the floor as they did so. Every single one of them was mooing loudly.

'Keep going, lads,' cried George, as he took another deep breath. His plan to attract the attention of the Reptilians was…

CLICK

…working.

The latch to the far entrance popped up and the door swung open. Two Draco guards had been sent to check out the noise and they looked very unhappy about it. Then again, their mean and ugly faces always looked nasty, so it was hard to tell. Either way, the first part of George's plan had worked.

'Hold,' urged George.

The Reptilians strode purposely into the hangar and cows continued to moo. The guards checked around the animals' holding cell, puzzled by their behaviour.

'Hold,' hissed George again. The Reptilians were closer now but not close enough. The boys were crouched in the corner of their cell. All of the straw had been pushed out through the bars onto the central walkway. The metal plates on the floor were now exposed.

'HOLD,' he said one last time. The guards finally turned and walked across to the boys' cage. 'Time to get angry.' And George jumped up, holding the metal dog bowl, and slammed it against the bars. The clanging echoed around the hangar.

Ben was just as fast. He leapt up and began kicking the bars are wildly as he could. They rattled and shook in their fixtures, the stainless steel clanging sharply with every boot.

Stan-Ley wasn't wearing shoes, he only had thin, almost invisible slippers made from Kevlar. He certainly did not enjoy the thought of breaking his toes on the bars, so instead he began jumping up and down on the metal plates that served as the floor. Now clear of straw, the panels bounced and vibrated with every wild leap. This clanking noise was deeper but just as loud.

Together, their beats created an enormous wall of sound; low and bass, higher and sharper, with the ear-piercing clash of the dog bowl on the bars. Imagine a cross between a large tambourine and an even bigger drum, the bowl din shattered the air around them.

George began running up and down the cell, dragging the bowl across all the bars at once. The racket was enough to annoy anyone and even Ben felt sickened by the bedlam they'd created.

But the Reptilians felt more than sick. Both guards doubled over, pressing their claws across their tiny ears and holding their eyes tight shut. They grimaced in pain, as the sound vibrations ripped over their eardrums.

'It's working!' yelled Stan-Ley above the clattering.

'What's working?' screeched Ben, still kicking at the bars.

George stopped rattling his dog bowl. Ben stopped kicking the cage and Stan-Ley stopped jumping and stood perfectly still, staring at George. Silence descended upon the hangar but the ringing still echoed in their ears.

'I don't know,' he whispered. George suddenly realised that he hadn't thought his plan through properly. Maybe he hoped to steal the keys from the guards. Maybe he just wanted to annoy them, to feel a little bit of control again. But the guards didn't seem to carry keys and they were too far away to search them.

And they were now getting to their feet. One of the lizard-men opened the gate to their cell with a touch of a keypad and the door swung outwards. Teeth were bared, eyes were red and blazing, and a thin thread of drool hung down over the green scaly skin.

George could think of nothing else but to rattle his dog bowl on the bars once more. This was too much for the guards. The first Reptilian reached behind his back and pulled out a large and vicious-looking blaster pistol. Red lights flickered along the barrel, and the weapon let out a soft little beep.

The Reptilian looked angrier than ever. His buddy was staring at him, perhaps there was thought-transfers or telepathy going on, but the furious lizard was not backing down. He lifted the pistol and aimed it straight at George.

Then fired!

Just as the trigger was being pulled, Stan-Ley leapt forward and pushed George to safety. A bright red beam of laser light shot past the boys and blasted into the wall behind them. Sparks burst out everywhere and shards of metal flew in every direction. Smoke billowed from the target and then slowly cleared.

The explosion had ripped a hole in the hull of the spacecraft and the brilliant blue sky shone in from beyond.

"Yeah, I can fly!"

Tony Stark (Iron Man)

Chapter 31 - Signs

Everyone in the control room turned and ran across to the view-window. A large ball of orange flames had erupted from the edge of the huge black spaceship. Large chunks of metal were falling to the ground and smoke billowed from the gaping hole.

The Greys' flying saucer had been hovering above the Dracos' craft, dwarfed in size but had the advantage of invisibility, thanks to their cloaking device. The distance between the two ships was only about three miles.

'That's the sign I wanted,' yelled Grandpa Jock, shuffling across to the window as fast as his webbed legs could carry him. 'Dorian, where's your exit? I need to get off this ship.'

Dorian held his hand open, inviting Grandpa Jock to the door on the right. The old Scotsman stumbled and staggered towards the doorway, grabbing at pod-chairs and children to keep his balance. Progress was going to be slow...

...until Dorian stepped forward and swooped Grandpa Jock off his feet, iron suit and all. The alien was tall but had long, spindly arms and legs. Yet, he was incredibly strong. They marched out of the control room and along the corridor.

'Hey,' smiled Grandpa Jock. 'What about non-contact?'

Dorian just nodded until they had reached the pod-bay doors. He set Grandpa Jock down and flashed his fingers across the shiny panel on the wall. The doorway swooshed open and the blue sky was exposed in front of them. The Reptilians' triangular craft sat below them, hovering above a small town.

'That's Little Pumpington,' yelled Kenny, running up behind the alien. 'And look at all the lights.' Barbara and Allison crowded around behind him. On the ground below, it seemed like hundreds of blue lights were flashing. A massive crowd had gathered and thousands of faces were peering upwards.

'They cannot see us,' said Dorian calmly.

'But they can see that big beggar across there,' grunted Grandpa Jock, staring out into the open space below.

'Jock, this ship is 5,000 metres away from the Dracos',' Dorian explained. 'We are positioned at an altitude 1,000 metres above them. The ground is a further 3,000 metres below that. Are you sure you want to do this?'

'Sometimes you've just got to run before you can walk,' shrugged Grandpa Jock, calmly. 'Or at least float before you can fly.'

He shuffled to the edge of the platform and stared over at the sudden drop beneath him. The ground looked a sickeningly long way down and Grandpa Jock felt his stomach lurch.

'Now, those people on the ground will be able to see you as soon as you step out of our cloaking device,' Dorian went on. 'As if you have just appeared from thin air.'

'I'm no' worried aboot the people, Dorian. It's the ground itself that I'm bothered aboot. It looks kinda solid doon there.' Grandpa Jock's voice quivered, as he reached up to pull his mask down. He winked back at the children, just before it covered his face.

'Don't try this at home, kids!' Grandpa Jock adjusted his headphones, lifted his left leg, farted, then threw himself out of the saucer and into the abyss.

> *"You can't come to any harm when you're falling. It's the landing part you have to worry about."*
>
> **Danger Mouse**

'Jock! Jock! Can you hear me, Jock.' Dorian was back in the control room, shouting into the microphone on the desk. 'Push the button on your belt, Jock.'

There was a sharp crackle, as static rippled through the speakers, then a deafening blast of bagpipe music. Everyone in the control room jumped back and covered their ears, before the music was cut and a voice echoed out of the speakers…

'Erm… sorry aboot that. I just pressed the wrong button.'

'How are you doing, Jock?' Dorian was sliding his fingers across the touchscreen furiously. 'We have you clocked at 200 miles per hour, Jock. How are you holding up?'

'I'm not holding up… I'm falling down!' Grandpa Jock screamed, and the voice in his headphones came back… 'Help!'

'Spread your arms and legs out wide, Jock. Like a kite…'

Grandpa Jock stretched his arms out and the flaps caught the wind. At the same time, he opened his feet apart and the thermal currents grabbed the three Kevlar triangles of material. He stopped falling down and started gliding forwards.

'I can fly!' screamed the old fella, relieved, mainly because he was no longer plummeting downwards.

'That is better, Jock. You have slowed your descent.'

Dorian was speaking slowly too, trying to keep the old geezer calm. 'You jumped from our saucer as it hovered, so that is different from exiting a moving aircraft. Therefore, your initial airspeed upon exit was absent. Your vertical drop used the forces of gravity to accelerate, generating airspeed. The wings on your suit are now generating lift.'

'I can fly!'

Another voice came over Grandpa Jock's headset, much higher and much, much more excited... 'You go, Iron-Bru-Man!'

> ## "Why do we fall? So we can learn to pick ourselves back up."
> **Batman**

Grandpa Jock grinned. He tucked his chin down against his chest and felt the force of momentum wobble his false teeth in the wind. After his initial drop, he was almost gliding level now, flying headlong into the sky. The Dracos' ship, which had seemed tiny to begin with, was now starting to look bigger beyond his goggles.

His moustache was whipping around the sides of his face and tufts of ginger hair were being blown back behind his mask-strap. At one point, old Jock shook his head to flick hair from the front of his mask, and he discovered that if he dropped his left shoulder, he swooped down to the left. Then, he dropped his right shoulder, and sure enough, he glided in the opposite direction.

Testing his new techniques, Grandpa Jock pulled his feet together and he suddenly shot forwards and downwards like a bullet, increasing velocity at an alarming rate. His heart missed a beat and he pulled his feet apart again quickly, so he levelled off and flew straight again. The signs were looking good.

Closer.

His main problem now was the wet kilt behind the Kevlar fabric between his legs and wrapped underneath his second skin of Iron Brew cans. The damp material was getting very cold and he could feel the circulation slowing down beneath his knees. Grandpa Jock started wiggling his toes furiously inside his boots to keep them warm.

Closer!

The Reptilian ship was growing larger and larger as the tin-man flew in closer and closer. It hung there in the sky, as if suspended by invisible thread. Ripples of power fizzed out from beneath the craft and Grandpa Jock guessed that was the anti-gravity emissions Dorian had told him about many years ago.

Many governments around the world had had anti-gravity power for decades but chose not to use it. Instead, the powers-that-be were happy to continue burning fossil fuels, as long as it made them more money.

CLOSER!!

Focus Jock, he whispered to himself and targeted the hole in the side of the craft, dropping his right shoulder to adjust his direction. The hole was still smouldering slightly and the black entrance was his bullseye.

It was at this point that Grandpa Jock realised he did not know how to stop his Wing-Suit. The flying part was straight forward enough, the falling part was dead easy but the stopping part now seemed very difficult. Dead easy? That's not a good choice of words, he thought.

And why was it called a dead end? Was he about to meet his? Dorian's voice suddenly cut through clear and keen into his headphones...

'We have you on radar, Jock. Your speed is down to just seventy miles an hour.' *JUST* thought Grandpa Jock. 'Get ready to pull back. Pull back your head, push your legs forward and spread your arms as wide as you can. This will act like a brake against your windspeed.'

'In three, two…' The hole in the side of the ship was almost on top of him now.

'ONE'

Grandpa Jock pushed his head back and felt the air pressure on his mask. His arms were almost ripped backwards out of their sockets. His toes were pointed forward to make a perfectly balanced landing through the gaping hole until…

Three small boys stepped into the gap! Well, two small boys and a smaller grey alien. Effectively, one black kid, one white kid and one grey kid… a little monochrome barrier to a safe landing.

Arms, legs, heads, wings… everything went tumbling in a jumble of body parts backwards into the prison cell. Then more arms, legs, heads and green scales joined the rolling ball of bodies through the cell gate and into the hangar.

"You know, I guess one man can make a difference. 'Nuff said."

Stan 'The Man' Lee - Spiderman 3

Chapter 32 - Independence Hour

Grandpa Jock was the first to recover. He gave his head a little shake, waggled his fingers and then wiggled his toes. *All in working order*, he thought. And he looked about him.

Initially, George, Ben and Stan-Ley had broken his fall. The two Reptilians had then broken their fall… and the bundle of bodies, half of them human, half of them alien, were now piled up beyond the cell door, next to a large cage of cows. The boys were beginning to come to.

'Grandpa…' groaned George, trying to untangle himself from the mass of arms, legs and aliens. Ben and Stan were also crawling out of the intergalactic game of *Twister*, looking slightly dazed but none the worse for wear. The Reptilians seemed to have taken the brunt of the damage. They were still lying spark out cold on the floor.

'Neat moves, Mr J,' sang Stan-Ley, as he finally stood up. 'Those lizard-dudes didn't see that one coming!'

'What do you mean *those lizard-dudes*?' laughed Ben. 'WE didn't see him coming either.'

'No time to waste, lads. We need to get out of here quickly.' Grandpa Jock was already on his feet and pulling out a thin, nylon cord from within the folds of his iron suit. It seemed to unwind for several metres before he looped it off in a fancy knot.

'Hold on, Mr Jock dude,' Stan-Ley interrupted. Grandpa Jock, George and Ben stopped and stared at him. Getting off the Reptilian ship was high on their priorities list. 'Those reptoids are still planning to take over your planet, man. This may be your one chance to stop them.'

At that moment, the speaker on the front of Grandpa Jock's suit crackled into life and Dorian's voice came across clearly. 'We have been monitoring your progress, Jock. Young Stan may have a point.'

'You are on board a Reptilian vessel with over two hundred

heavily armed Draco lizards,' Dorian continued. 'The ship's armour will protect them from anything your militaries can throw at them. Their weapons are hideously powerful. Humanity may not get another chance like this again.'

'There's no one else who can save the human race, Mr J.,' Stan-Ley shrugged. 'Once they've set up their base on Earth, more Reptilian ships will arrive. There might be thousands of them, and they will spread out across the Earth. They intend to crush, kill and capture every man, woman and child on your planet. Holy shizzle-sticks, dude… Dinner will definitely be served.'

Grandpa Jock was nodding slowly, a grim realisation setting across his features. Ben and George were exchanging glances, their desire to escape overtaken by their determination to save the world. George spoke first…

'We can do this, Grandpa,' he urged.

'The Earth won't be saved without a little sacrifice.' Ben was gritting his teeth.

'You have to be sure, Jock.' Stan-Ley held his hand out, staring firmly into the old Scotsman's face, searching for the truth. 'Tell me, why do you want to kill the lizard-men?'

Grandpa Jock replied, 'I don't want to kill anyone… **I just don't like bullies.**'

'We think we have found their weakness,' hissed George. 'But I don't know how to turn it into our advantage.'

'And it's gonna take a lot more than banging our dog bowl against the bars,' added Ben.

'Dog bowls? Whit are you talking aboot, laddie?' Grandpa Jock looked puzzled, until the boys explained the Reptilians' sensitive hearing and how they'd almost escaped by over-powering their guards with noise. Grandpa Jock's moustache rippled and a huge grin spread across his face.

'Crayon Kenny, I could kiss you!' laughed Grandpa Jock, and both Ben and George looked a little disgusted… and puzzled. Kenny was still across on the Greys' ship and the lads had no idea how he could help from away across there. Grandpa Jock reached around and flicked the switch on the battery pack attached to his belt. The light on his chest torch came on with a blue glow and soft bagpipe music began to play.

'Forgot that I turned the volume doon earlier, when I was talking to your dad.' Grandpa Jock was looking at Stan-Ley but still fumbling with the buttons on his head-set. The music was growing louder with every click of the button. The glowing speaker on his chest started to throb. Bagpipe music isn't just for the ears; it's music for your whole body.

Ben and Stan-Ley covered their own ears but George was used to this. He'd heard his grandpa playing his tunes at home hundreds of times. And he knew it was about to get louder.

Eeeeoowwwweeeyyeeeeooooohhhheeeyyyooooowwww!

'It sounds like a cat being tortured. It's horrible,' cried Stan-Ley, trying to make himself heard above the droning, whining racket. The shrieking, squealing din started getting louder. The air trembled as the noise became unbearable and Ben felt his tummy rumble with a rhythmic pounding.

'I'm jist gettin' warmed up,' laughed Grandpa Jock, walking across to the two lizard-men still lying in a heap on the floor. With a swift boot to each butt, he kicked the aliens and they began to awaken.

Although instantly they wished they hadn't. They pressed their hands across their little ears and winced in pain. Their heads were shaking, as they lost control and they began slapping their heads. Grandpa Jock flicked the volume up to eleven on the dial. The music was blasting out of his chest and…

What happened next can only be described as if you've filled a balloon with slimy, green gunge and blown it up as big as possible and then slapped it hard with both hands. That balloon would naturally explode.

Well, that's what happened to the two lizard-men. Exploded! Their bodies slumped, green slime oozing from the hole that had once been their heads. It was splattered over the floor. It was splattered over the cows. It was splattered over George, Ben and Stan-Ley. Grandpa Jock had suspected the worst and had stepped back carefully. He was unscathed by the green goo.

Unused to noise for decades, the sound vibrations from the bagpipes had simply caused the alien brains to spontaneously combust.

(Hello little reader, I know that the words to spontaneously combust are maybe a little beyond your vocabulary but they are such great words. Spontaneous means sudden, unexpected and impulsive. Combust means to explode or to burst. Think about that balloon again, and you keep blowing and blowing and blowing. It will go POP! at some point. Say it again…

Spon - tane - e - us -ly   Kom - bust

There… once you've said, now you own it!)

Grandpa Jock clicked the volume down and stepped forward. He giggled when he saw how much brain goo covered the boys. They were dripping in it.

'You three get yourselves cleaned up. I'll be back soon.'

And the old Scotsman, still unable to walk properly with the Kevlar mesh between his knees, raised himself up onto his toes and twinkled like a ballerina straight out of the hangar.

"The definition of
a hero is someone
concerned about other
people's well-being and
will go out of his or
her way to help them
– even with no chance
of a reward.
That person who helps
others simply because
it should or must be
done, and because it is
the right thing to do, is
indeed without a doubt,
a real superhero."

Stan Lee - Comic book writer, editor, publisher, producer, legend.

Chapter 33 - Predator

You don't really need to know what happened next, little reader, you are far too nice. But rest assured it was pretty gruesome. As the bagpipe music blared throughout Grandpa Jock's tour of the Reptilian battle cruiser, it was accompanied by soggy bangs, gooey blasts and squelchy pops. And there was slime... lots and lots of slime.

Once or twice the Dracos tried to fight back but the noise was just too dreadful to bear. They couldn't see straight... they couldn't shoot straight... and seconds later, their brains exploded straight out of their heads... all over the nearest wall.

The tables had been turned on these vicious killers, and Grandpa Jock stalked their ship like a fearless predator, the sound of bagpipes blasting from his chest speaker. The two hundred reptoids were no match for his mad music. It was a gooey, green snot-fest! And eventually, the kilted hitman finally made his way back to the cow hangar.

George, Ben and Stan-Ley had just about been able to wipe off most of the reptile brains from their clothes when Grandpa Jock marched in. The music was switched off now, and the old geezer was dripping in green brain goo. His Iron-Bru-Man metal suit was absolutely covered from head to toe in gunge and the slime dripped off him in sloppy big lumps.

'Do you need a tissue, Grandpa?' George called over, giggling. 'You look like you've sneezed.'

'I wish it was snot,' groaned Grandpa Jock. 'This brain stuff stinks.'

'Here, use some straw to wipe off the worst of it,' said Ben, passing Grandpa Jock a handful. 'Stan, give him some more. Stan. Stan?'

The small grey alien had turned towards the gaping hole in the side of the Reptilian ship. His eyes were screwed up tight and his fingers were dancing lightly.

'Telepathy,' nodded Grandpa Jock. 'I've seen this before. His dad must be sending him a message.'

It must have been a long message because Stan-Ley stood there for another four or five minutes, sometimes perfectly still, other times letting his fingers flicker across his thighs, his eyelids fluttering back and forth. Sending and receiving.

Eventually he stood bolt upright, opened his large black eyes to their fullest and turned towards the three humans. 'Ben, grab two of those cow harnesses,' Stan-Ley commanded, his laid-back boyish charm gone and an air of seriousness descended. 'George, give him a hand.'

'Mr J. I need to make this quick,' Stan-Ley continued abruptly. 'My dad says that a large crowd has gathered below. They are watching, and filming, an enormous black triangular craft, believed to be of extraterrestrial origin. Your social media has gone into meltdown.'

'Viral,' whispered George and Ben together.

'They can't see our saucer but people can certainly see this ship,' nodded Stan-Ley. 'My dad says I have to pilot it out of here… into orbit.'

'You can fly,' gasped George.

'Well, I've had one or two lessons. How hard can it be, right?' Stan-Ley gulped. Acting serious was simply his way of fighting off an attack of nerves. 'And anyway, you humans just can't get hold of the Dracos weapons. You are bad enough with your own.'

He marched over to Ben and took the first harness out of his hands and began clipping and connecting different buckles.

'Many people below have also caught you on camera, Mr J., when you jumped out of the flying saucer. The ship was cloaked so you looked as if you appeared from nowhere, dude.' Stan-Ley spoke without looking up. He looped the first harness up and over Ben's head and shoulders, then did the same with George. Lastly, he clipped the combined harness straps onto the nylon line streaming out of the Iron-Bru-Man suit.

'You're ready,' nodded Stan. Grandpa Jock bobbed his head, knowing exactly what he had to do.

'Ready for what, Grandpa?' asked George, with a little quiver in his voice.

Grandpa Jock just smiled and stepped towards the gaping hole, dragging the two boys behind him. 'He's flying this ship into space, and we're jumping out here. Remember kids, don't try this at home.'

And with that, he leapt out into the open air, whisking George and Ben with him. Their screams were deafening.

> *"We're not alone. There are life forms out there, which while they are not hostile, have clearly shown that they're not pleased with our tendency to put weapons in space."*
>
> **Dr Steven M. Greer, MD – Director, The Disclosure Project**

'AAARRRGGGHHH!' screamed George.

'AAARRRGGGHHH!' screamed Ben, at exactly the same time.

They screamed until all the air was blown out of their lungs, and they were forced to take in another deep breath. Then they started screaming again.

'AAAAAARRRRRRGGGGGGGHHHHH!' they screamed together.

Then the screaming stopped and the only noise was the rushing in their ears as they plummeted towards the ground. Except... they weren't falling downwards. They were falling forwards, pulled along behind Grandpa Jock's BASE jumping suit. He was bobbing and weaving, dropping one shoulder then the other in a gradual, slowed descent. He was in control. Actually, George thought, Grandpa Jock was beginning to enjoy himself.

'You've stopped screaming,' shouted Ben, trying make himself heard over the rushing wind.

'So have you,' yelled George.

'It's not too bad when you stop panicking. Look!' Ben was pointing upwards and George was just able to turn his head to see the huge spaceship spin 180 degrees, lights flashing all around the base. The alien craft jerked forward, then stalled. Then jerked forwards again and wobbled. Finally, the spaceship spun around once more and swept majestically upwards at an incredible speed. Within seconds the flying object was gone.

'I hope he gives the cows a good home,' yelled George, his eyes still fixed in the distance.

'Never mind the cows, George,' shouted Ben, pointing down this time. The ground was rushing up to meet them as they whizzed forwards and downwards.

'I JUST HOPE WE LAND SAFELY!'

"But why the Moon? Why choose this as our goal? And they may well ask, why climb the highest mountain? Why, 35 years ago, fly the atlantic? We choose to go to the Moon! We choose to go to the Moon in this decade and do the other things, not because they are easy, but because they are hard; because that goal will serve to organise and measure the best of our energies and skills, because that challenge is one that we are willing to accept, one we are unwilling to postpone, and one we intend to win!"

**John F. Kennedy - 12th September 1962
- 35th President of the United States**

Chapter 34 - Thor One

The trio sailed through the air, gliding over the heads of most of the population of Little Pumpington who had turned out to witness the massive black UFO that had, until a few moments ago, been hovering above their town.

Most of them had their mobile phones out, holding them up and filming the spectacular events in the sky. UFOs, explosions and a strange, robotic man, dragging what looked like two small boys behind him. Was he a superhero? Was he an alien? Certainly not a bird or a plane!

Dozens of police officers, who were meant to be holding the crowds back, had stopped to watch the action. There was even a television crew from LPTV (Little Pumpington Television) set up on top of the band stand in the corner of the parade ground.

Actually, it wasn't really a parade ground, as such. It was more of a grassy car park, next to a football pitch, alongside a large patch of wasteland. The ground was a mixture of bone-dry red ash and soggy puddles. Even in the hottest weather the mud there just never dried up. And, like most patches of grass in every town, there were lots of little piles of dog poo. Stan-Ley was right.

The film crew had a great view of the gliding man as he swooped over the grass, two or three metres above the ground. Suddenly, the iron-clad geezer, his suit glinting in the sunshine, pulled backwards, going almost vertical. His momentum slowed and for a split second he seemed to hover in the air.

His passengers swooped beneath him, landing gently in a heap on the grass. But now, with no forward motion or air speed, gravity kicked in. The man dropped to the ground like a stone, landing on his face. His iron fist was next to touch down and plumes of dust flew up. Breaking his fall with his mouth was not a good idea.

'Thor!' cried Grandpa Jock, bouncing to his feet, his tin suit clanking. 'Thor, thor, thor!' he squealed, as the camera team rushed forward. Police and people were flocking towards the band stand area from all over the parade ground. George and Ben backed up the steps to get away from the mob, dragging the still-dazed Grandpa Jock with them.

'Who are you?' someone shouted.

'Where did you come from?' yelled another voice.

'I think he said his name was Thor?' added another.

Grandpa Jock stood at the top of the band stand steps and turned towards the boys. He flipped the goggle mask up and stuck his tongue out at the lads. A spot of blood was starting to pool on the tip of his tongue.

'Tho thor,' he lisped. 'I landed on my faith... bit my thong.' George and Ben sniggered together, as the old Scotsman wiped the speck of blood onto the back of his metal glove.

The television crew pushed closer, and a camera was thrust into Grandpa Jock's face, followed by a large microphone. He pulled his goggle mask back down over his eyes, as the sound engineer flicked the loud speakers on.

'We saw you appear... from nowhere... in the sky. You flew into that... that... that spaceship. We have footage,' spat the TV reporter. 'Can you confirm that you are an alien?'

'Thorry, ith thill thoo thor.'

'That's an alien language alright,' gasped the cameraman, his eyes popping out of his head at his first glimpse on a real 'ET'.

'Did you come in peace or are you here to take over the world? Where has your spaceship gone? Will they be coming back for you? Which planet do you come from?Do you speak English?' The reporter was firing question after question at Grandpa Jock without waiting for an answer. 'Can you confirm your name is Thor?'

In that second, Grandpa Jock had a moment of pure clarity. Dorian had said that the footage of his appearance and the alien ship had gone viral. Most likely he was now live on television, on the internet and across social media. The crowd was split between taking photos one moment to tapping out a post or a tweet or sharing a video the next. Most likely, the whole world was watching.

This was his big chance.

'Yeth,' he lisped again, looking directly into the camera. 'My name ith Thor… Valiant Thor and I have returned.' George could see people in the crowd tapping that name into Google on their phones.

'Many yearsth ago I came to Earth, to help humankind. But it wath not enough. And now orbiting the Earth, I have theen the damage you are doing to your world,' Grandpa Jock went on. The crowd was hushed into total silence.

'You need to have a shared vision of change. You need to create a world that is fit for generations to come. You are living in a toxic system but no one individual is to blame. Your planet Earth has hit the skids and climate change is killing your kids.'

With the pain in his tongue subsiding, Grandpa Jock began speaking clearer and with more urgency.

'I don't say this to scare you but the Earth has reached a tipping point and you must act swiftly. Cut back on the meat you eat. Plant more trees… plant a billion trees. Heck, plant seven billion trees! Stop flying so much and stop burning fossil fuels.'

George looked across the parade ground and he could just make out Barbara, Crayon Kenny and Allison cutting their way through the crowd, coming towards them.

'I believe there is a hero in all of us. And when you decide not to be afraid, you will find friends in super unexpected places.' Grandpa Jock thrust his shoulders back. 'Climate change is occurring earlier and more rapidly than you expected. And now you must all be Superheroes and Super-sheroes. You need to become Superheroes to save the planet. No one else will do it for you.'

Whilst Grandpa Jock was in the middle of his speech, George and Ben stepped down from the band stand to meet the other three. George almost hugged Allison, he was so delighted to see that they were safe but he saw Kenny's disapproving look so he just high-fived everyone instead.

'We were on a freaking spaceship,' Barbara babbled.

'Yeah,' groaned Ben. 'They stink, don't they.'

'No way, bro! Ours was amazing. Anti-gravity, zero carbon emissions, and invisibility. And check out their cool uniforms.' Barbara was still wearing Kevlar spacesuit.

'Yeah, pretty neat,' agreed Ben. 'And if I'm the Black Puma, you must be Shuri.'

'Shuri not,' giggled Kenny but nobody else joined in. A good line wasted!

'But if you were up there,' puzzled George. 'How did you get down here?'

'Dorian kept the invisibility cloak on and drop us off on the wasteland over there,' replied Allison, pointing across.

'What about the other dude?' asked Ben. 'That Nick Poop guy? Where's he now?'

'He's still on board the spaceship. Said it was his dream come true,' laughed Kenny. 'He doesn't want to leave... even asked if he could stay. Take me with you, he was yelling. If they try to drag him off he'll be kicking and screaming all the way.'

'Talking of kicking and screaming, Mr Jock seems to be in full flow up there,' Allison nodded towards the band stand. Grandpa Jock had grabbed the microphone from the reporter and was now strutting across the stage.

'Methane and carbon are killing the planet,' he shouted into the mic. 'Cut out fossil fuels and cut back on cow farts. Buy local foods that have a low carbon footprint.'

But he felt his words were lacking power.

Then he remembered something spoken a long time ago.

A speech used to create a shared vision, a goal and a very specific mission. A task that brought together hundreds of thousands of people. Grandpa Jock took a deep breath.

'The hazards are hostile to us all. The conquest of climate change deserves the best of all mankind, and its opportunity for peaceful cooperation may never come again,' he paused dramatically. 'But why, some say, tackle climate change? Why choose this as our goal? And they may well ask, why climb the highest mountain? Why, 50 years ago, go to the moon? Why tackle Climate Change?'

'We choose to overcome this Climate Catastrophe! We choose to overcome this Climate Catastrophe in this decade, not because it is easy, but because it is hard; because that goal will serve to organise and measure the best of our energies and skills, to maintain this planet and save the human race. This challenge is one that we are willing to accept, one we are unwilling to postpone, and one we intend to win!'

Grandpa Jock spread his arms out wide. He lifted his Kevlar wings up and dropped the mic on the floor with a sonic **BOOM!** He pointed his fingers to the sky, hoping, indeed expecting, to receive a standing ovation from the crowd.

But... just whining feedback from the microphone screeched through the speakers... and one or two people in the crowd coughed. It was dry enough for tumbleweed but none blew across the stage. Just a breeze whistling gently through the trees.

Iron-Bru-Man, or Valiant Thor, or just plain old Grandpa Jock had said his piece, his commitment to change and his call to action but it felt like no one was listening. Perhaps his message was too big to grasp? Maybe human brains are too small to deal with such a huge threat. Planet Earth doesn't come with a user manual and he had paralysed the audience into stunned silence.

Now Grandpa Jock just stood quietly on the stage all alone for what seemed like an eternity.

The crowd slowly began to disperse with puzzled looks on their faces, checking the photos and videos on their phones again and again. Alien or not? The TV reporter picked the microphone up without a word and the cameraman switched off the camera.

Still dressed in their own superhero outfits; Stink-King, Black Puma, Miss Marvel, the Ginger Ninja and Shuri, all shuffled away from the stage.

Barbara sighed. 'Maybe it will sink in soon. Maybe someday people will realise.'

'Before it's too late…' Ben and Kenny whispered together.

'Still Guardians of the Garden?' asked Allison.

George shook his head. 'No, it's bigger than that… we are the guardians of the whole world now.'

The End

"We're running out of time but there is still hope."

Sir David Attenborough OM CH CVO CBE FRS FLS FZS FSA FRSGS*
Broadcaster and natural historian. April 2019

Intelligent Lifeforms in Our Galaxy

The Venusians

This species come from the planet Venus and in many ways, look much like any human on the Earth.

They are described as being tall, usually over 6 feet, solidly built and have dark hair.

Valiant Thor was the first Venusian to land on planet Earth.

The Venusians are said to be handsome, with piercing blue eyes. They have six fingers on each hand, an oversized heart, one very large lung, copper oxide blood, and an estimated IQ of 1200 (the average human IQ is 100). Plus, they can speak 100 languages, walk through walls, and have a lifespan of 500 years.

The Greys

The Greys are from a planet in the Zeta Reticula systems, approx. 39 light years from Earth. They have oversized heads, large black almond-shaped eyes, no visible ears and little slit mouths.

Their skin is smooth and pale grey in colour. They are completely hairless and they have three fingers on each hand. They are between one and two metres tall, with thin arms and legs.

It has been suggested that the Greys influenced the evolution of life on Earth in the distant past. Specifically that ETs were directly involved in the genetic engineering of primates to artificially create humans.

The Nordics

The "Nordics" are an alien race from the Pleiades star cluster, located 444 light years from Earth. They are so-called Nordic due to their Scandinavian features; blue eyes, long blond hair and pale, milky white skin.

They are very tall, often over two metres in height, and communicate through telepathy, which is like hearing a person but they're not actually speaking. It is said that the Nordics have a lifespan of almost 500 years.

The Nordics have been described as "paternal, watchful, smiling, affectionate, and youthful".

The Reptilians

The Reptilians are a vicious, war-like species of blood-drinking, flesh-eating shape-shifters, originally from the Alpha Draconis star system. They spread out across the galaxy millennia ago, with one colony finally landing and hiding in an underground base on the dark side of the moon. They have four digits on each claw; three fingers and one opposable thumb.

Their skin is green and scaly, and their eyes have vertical, slit pupils. Although their heads are small, this species has a well-developed brain and the ability take on human form. This is done by projecting holographic vibrations into the human mind.

The Reptilians are aggressive, brutal and single-minded. They harbour savage, primitive desires to satisfy their hunger, thirst and greed for territory.

Reptilian extinction was almost brought about through their limited and short-sighted thinking, which resulted in planetary-wide climate change, overpopulation, overconsumption and the rapid decrease in the biodiversity of their home planet.

The Reptilians are also known as Dracos, Reptoids or Lizard People.

The Humans

Human beings originated on Earth, in Africa approximately 315,000 years ago, venturing out to populate most of the planet.

Humans can be recognised by their erect posture, bipedal movement and high manual dexterity, and heavy tool use, with their four fingers and one opposable thumb. Their open-ended language use is much more complex than other Earthly animal communications. They have more complex brains than other animals on Earth and have created highly advanced (by Earth standards) and organised societies.

The spread of this large and increasing population of humans has affected much of the biosphere of their planet and decimated millions of species worldwide.

Humans are capable of abstract reasoning, problem solving and culture, understanding science and creating technologies, literature, music and fine art.

Despite their artistic and creative abilities, humans are a violent species, almost continually involved in lethal conflicts throughout their history. Wars and military campaigns between at least two opposing sides have taken place for thousands of years, usually involving a dispute over sovereignty, territory, resources, and religion. In the last 3,400 years, humans have been entirely at peace for just 268 of them, or just 8 percent of recorded history.

Human extinction may happen as a result of human action, most likely brought about by man-made climate change, too many people, eating and using too many things and the widespread and rapid decrease in the number of different species on Earth.

Humans are the cause of the Earth's 6th Mass Extinction Event but have the intelligence and problem-solving skills to stop this destruction, if they so choose.

"The greatest power on Earth is the magnificent power we all possess... the power of the human brain!"

Professor Charles Xavier - X-Men

Acknowledgements

Massive thanks go to Nick Pope, former British Government Ministry of Defence official for all the information and ideas he provided. Thanks too, for sending the U.S. Department of Defense emails from US Senator Harry Reid, and to Senator John McCain, Chairman of the Senate Armed Services Committee, which revealed several highly sensitive, unconventional aerospace-related findings.

These declassified documents included research into Advanced Nuclear Propulsion for Manned Deep Space Missions, Advanced Space Propulsion based on Vacuum Engineering, Invisibility Cloaking, Traversable Wormholes, Stargates and Negative Energy, Antigravity for Aerospace Communications, Warp Drive, Dark Energy and the Manipulation of Extra Dimensions, Quantum Computing, and High Energy Laser Weapons, amongst other documents.

Nick is now an investigative journalist and commentator on television programmes such as Ancient Aliens and Alien Files Unsealed.

Credit is also given to George Carlin, comedian and social critic, for his inspiration with Chapter 21 in this book.

Abbreviations

Professor Stephen Hawking CH, CBE, FRS, FRSA*
* CH - Order of the Companions of Honour
* CBE - Commander of the British Empire
* FRS - Fellowship of the Royal Society
* FRSA - Fellowship of the Royal Society of Arts
Lord Dowding GCB, GCVO, CMG*- Air Chief Marshal in
British Royal Air Force. Air Command Officer RAF Fighter Command
* GCB - The Most Honourable Order of the Bath
* GCVO - The Royal Victorian Order for distinguished personal
  service to the monarch of the Commonwealth Realms.
* CMG - The Most Distinguished Order of St Michael and St George.
Sir David Attenborough OM CH CVO CBE FRS FLS FZS FSA FRSGS*
Broadcaster and natural historian.
* OM - The Order of Merit
* CH - The Order of Companions of Honour
* CVO - Royal Victorian Order
* CBE - The Most Excellent Order of the British Empire
* FRS - Fellowship of the Royal Society
* FLS - Fellow of the Linnean Society of London
* FZS - Fellow of the Zoological Society of London
* FSA - Fellow of the Society of Antiquaries of London
* FRSGS - Fellow of the Royal Scottish Geographical Society

About the author,
Stuart Reid

Stuart Reid is 52 years old, going on 10.

Throughout his early life he was dedicated to being immature, having fun and getting into trouble. After scoring a goal in the playground Stuart was known to celebrate by kissing lollypop ladies.

He is allergic to ties; blaming them for stifling the blood flow to his imagination throughout his twenties and thirties. After turning up at the wrong college, Stuart was forced to spend the next 25 years being boring, professional and corporate. His fun-loving attitude was further suppressed by the weight of career responsibility, as a business manager in the retail and hospitality industries in the UK and Dubai.

Stuart is one of the busiest authors in the world today, performing at schools, libraries and book festivals with his book events, *Reading Rocks!* He has appeared at over 2,000 schools since 2011, throughout Britain, Ireland, India, Abu Dhabi, Dubai, Hong Kong and Australia.

He won the Forward National Literature Silver Seal in 2012 for his debut novel, *Gorgeous George and the Giant Geriatric Generator.* Stuart's 7th book *Gorgeous George and the Timewarp Trouser Trumpets* won the silver medal at the Wishing Shelf Book Awards. He has also been presented with an Enterprise in Education Champion Award from Falkirk Council.

Stuart has been married to Audrey for over twenty-five years. He has two children, Jess and Charley, a spiky haircut and an awesome man-cave filled with cool stuff!

About the illustrator, John Pender

John is 39 and currently lives in Grangemouth with his wife Angela and their young son, Lucas, aged 8.

Working from his offices in Glasgow, John has been a professional graphic designer and illustrator since he was 18 years old, contracted to create illustrations, artwork and digital logos for businesses around the world, along with a host of individual commissions of varying degrees.

Being a comic book lover since the age of 4, illustration is his true passion, doodling everything from the likes of Transformers, to Danger Mouse to Spider-man and Batman in pursuit of honing his skills over the years.

As well as cartoon and comic book art, John is also an accomplished digital artist, specialising in a more realistic form of art for this medium, and draws his inspiration from acclaimed names such as Charlie Adlard, famous for The Walking Dead graphic novels, Glenn Fabry from the Preacher series, as well as the renowned Dan Luvisi, Leinil Yu, Steve McNiven and Gary Frank.

John has been married to Angela for 9 years and he describes his wife as his 'source of inspiration, positivity and motivation for life.' John enjoys the relaxation and stress-relief that family life can bring.

"Our kids' planet and their education is being so messed around, we need to help them make their voices heard."

"Climate devastation is an emergency. Nations must face up to that reality and activate emergency mindsets and call on institutions to act with national unity."

Farhana Yamin - Environmental Lawyer and Climate Change Development Policy Expert. A member of the Global Agenda Council on Climate Change at the World Economic Forum.